SLAVE OF ATLANTIS

BOOK ONE OF THE EPOS OF ATLANTIS

FENIX HARPER-JONES

Houten & Holleren

EDITIONS

SLAVE OF ATLANTIS
After the translation by
Royce B. E. Gibbons, CMG
retold by
Fenix Harper-Jones

ISBN 979-8-88722-833-4 (e-book)
ISBN 979-8-88722-834-1 (print)
Library of Congress Control Number
2022910789

Art by Ben Tripp

Published by
Houten & Holleren Editions
442 5th Avenue #1682
New York, NY 10018
United States of America
https://houtenandholleren.com/

*Dedicated to Dr. E. U. Graham,
gentleman and scholar.*

AUTHOR'S FOREWORD

What follows is a retelling of volume I of Royce E. Gibbons' classic translation of the *Epos of Atlantis*. For aeons, the *Epos* was an oral tradition. It may have included much of Atlantis' history. The *Epos* (or epic) takes place at least 35,000 years ago. It is the oldest story known to exist. All that remains today is a fragment. It tells of the legendary hero Tar Un Ka.

7,000 years ago, a transcript of Tar Un Ka's exploits was listed in the inventory of ruler Apt-Am (which is all that survives of Apt-Am's reign). Pisistratus the tyrant (600-527 BCE), who commissioned the first compilation of Homer's works, is said to have had a copy.

The only extant copy was discovered by Gibbons himself. It was part of the magnificent 3,600 year-old 'Lost Caravan' burial hoard, unearthed in the 1840s near Bukhara, Uzbekistan, during the course of the first and second Anglo-Sikh wars.

Gibbons dedicated the remainder of his life to translating the one hundred and twenty-three manuscripts in the treasure, about half of which contained the *Epos*. It was a monumental task. In a letter to his brother, Gibbons described the hoard's unique writing system as 'Proto-Indo-Aryan hen scratch'.

The first volume of his translation was privately published through Farber, Bell Academic Press in 1868; the tenth and final volume was never published, as the author died in 1889 with only a rough transliteration completed. A subsequent conflict between the publisher and Gibbons' estate meant no-one else was able to finish his opus. Farber, Bell went out of business after the Great War, and no subsequent effort was made to reprint the finished volumes or complete the final part. Until 1986, even Gibbons' working notes were forgotten, sealed away in the archives of Holy Cross College (Dublin).

Following the closure of that college in 2019, the late Fr. Pádraig Ó Suibhne made the full Gibbons archive available to the present author—including the unfinished final volume of the *Epos*. This retelling is owed entirely to Fr. Ó Suibhne's generosity.

Gibbons's version is a reflection of his influences. 18th century *Sturm und Drang*, early 19th century romantic poetry, and the Orientalist art movement fired his imagination. To spare the sensibilities of his Victorian audience, he bowdlerized the many violent, sexual, and morally dubitable passages of the original. Polygenists such as de Gobineau and Vogt also left their mark: The more sympathetic a character is in Gibbons' text, the more European they become—and vice-versa.

Finally, his rendering includes numerous mistranslations:

Gibbons—
    Rocs, with two human heads
    Original—
    Birds two men tall

In his defense, Gibbons was up against a difficult problem. The 'hen scratch' writing system was probably developed to record inventories, genealogies, and crop records—not epic tales. Consequently, there is no dialog in the original, only summaries of what was discussed. Story events are formatted as lists, which look ridiculous to the modern eye: Imagine a restaurant menu featuring detailed sexual liaisons and hand-to-hand combat.

The version before you is also a reflection of the author's influences. While the events and characters depicted in this telling are faithful to the original, much invention was necessary to fill them out. There is no denying the effect of movies, television, graphic novels and pop culture on that invention. If Gibbons' version seems quaint today, this update will seem quaint tomorrow. So it goes.

Given the sheer number of incidents in the complete cycle, it may be that the *Epos* was essentially a bronze-age crib sheet —something a storyteller would review prior to oration, rather than reciting directly off the page. According to this theory, the text was merely an austere outline, intended to be be expanded with dialog, action, and description by the narrator. It is in that spirit that the present adaptation was written.

Measurements such as weights and distances have been converted into roughly approximate imperial units. The identities of metals, such as bronze and steel, are conjectural. They may have been entirely different alloys. In the original they're named by color alone.

Many of today's animals didn't exist in Tar Un Ka's time. For example, there are no dogs mentioned in the entire *Epos*. Some have clear modern equivalents, such as camels and porpoises. Others, including giant three-finned sharks and umbrella-sized spiders, are likely to be inventions. Then again, the fossil record constantly yields surprises, such as *Kelenken guillermoi*, an improbably large hunting bird matching the description 'two men tall'. It replaces Gibbons' Roc.

There is no evidence of whom the Ancient Races were. They are said to have ruled all of the planet's inland territories, yet there is no physical trace of their existence—no artifacts or fossils of any kind. Most likely, these beings are apocryphal. The same can be said of the pithecines, dwargs, and similar quasi-human peoples in the story. However unlikely, it is pleasing to imagine they were survivals of *Gigantopithecus*, *Homo neanderthalensis*, and other long-vanished cousins of men.

Obverse view, gold coin
(before 5,500 BCE)

The map of the Atlantean empire is a hybrid. It is partially derived from a much later document that corresponds with the world described in the ancient text, and partially from our present understanding of geography prior to the most recent ice ages. The map of Atlantis itself is derived primarily from descriptions in the *Epos*. Some elements are borrowed from an ancient coin in the Iraq Museum, now lost, which was stamped with a design that may be a plan of Atlantis. A very few details are owed to Plato's dialogs *Timaeus* and *Critias*.

The Atlantis depicted here is a civilization of extremes. It is at once advanced and backward, ambitious and decadent, convinced of its own permanence even as it decays from within. Metal rots and stone turns to dust; mountains fall and seas rise. Everything is swept away. All that remains of Atlantis is legends.

It is hubris to imagine that our own civilization will fare any differently, given time. A hundred thousand years from now, it will be as if our history, language, art, architecture, and technology never existed.

If we follow the path of every civilization that has gone before, all that will remain of us is legends. This is nothing to despair about—of all humanity's creations, only legends defy the vastness of time. We will be remembered.

Fenix Harper-Jones
June 12, 2022

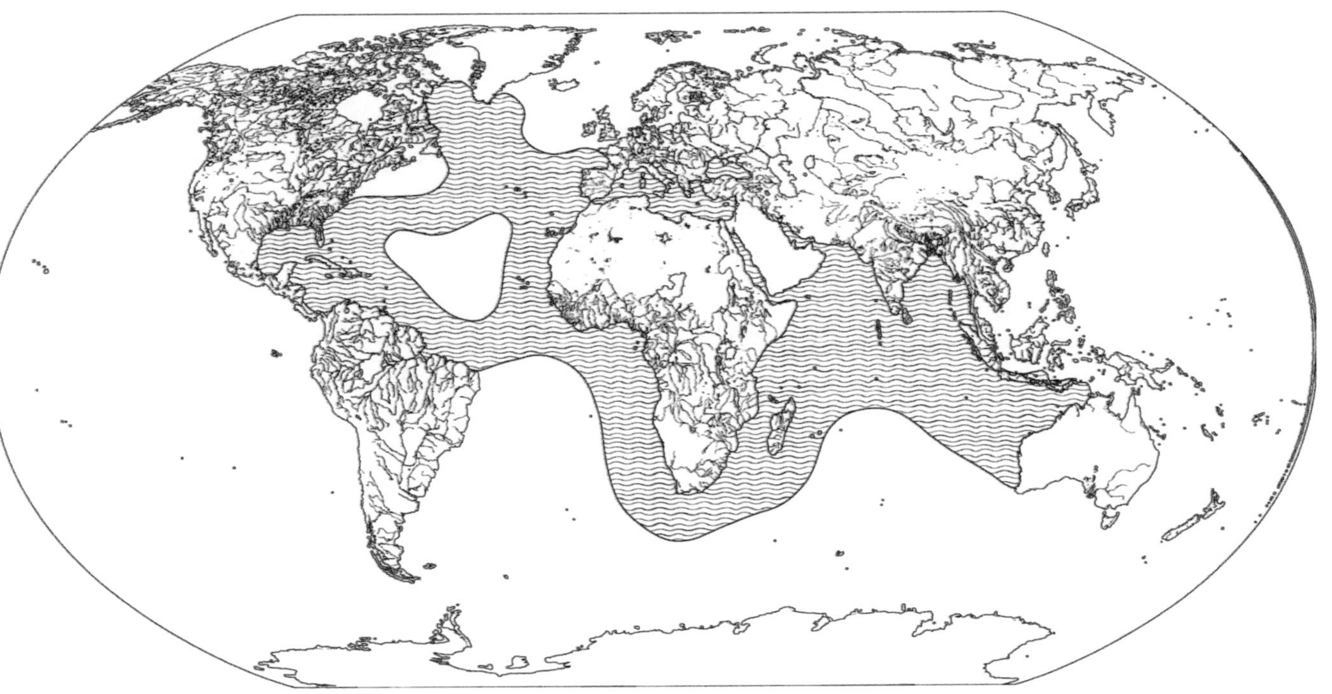

EXTENT OF SEA CONTROLLED BY THE ATLANTEAN EMPIRE
At peak of extent, 5th Dynasty (conjectural)

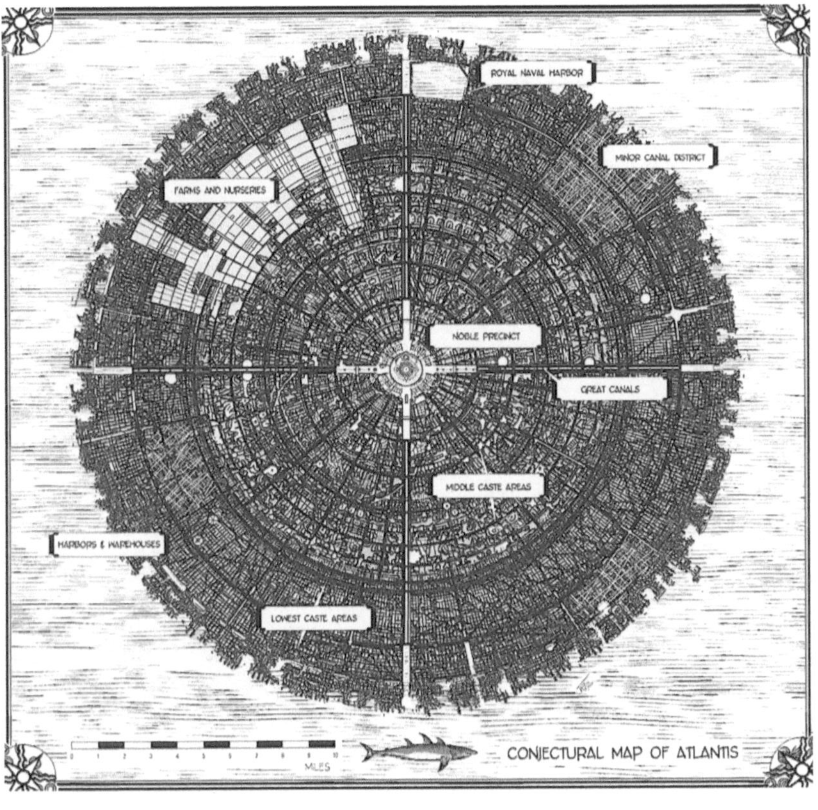

ROYAL NAVAL HARBOR
MINOR CANAL DISTRICT
FARMS AND NURSERIES
NOBLE PRECINCT
GREAT CANALS
MIDDLE CASTE AREAS
HARBORS & WAREHOUSES
LOWEST CASTE AREAS
0 1 2 3 4 5 6 7 8 9 10
MILES
CONJECTURAL MAP OF ATLANTIS

PROLOGUE TO THE EPOS OF ATLANTIS

(Translation by Royce E. Gibbons, CMG)

Long ago, before the creeping sea of ice
Thrice flowed down from the north
And swallowed up the world
Thinking beasts, fashioned
By ten thousand rival gods
Dwelt among the three continents.

These gods endowed their best creations
With gifts, that they might rule.
Some with tusk and fang and claw
Some with stealth and speed and prowess
Some with venom, treachery, and magic
Drownèd the continents in blood.

Long ago, before the creeping sea of ice
Thrice flowed down from the north
And swallowed up the world

Man, whose only gift was cunning
Raised a golden sea-borne citadel
That which no blood could drown, and ruled.

So was Atlantis born.

PART I

1

Ancient races ruled the land. They had no interest in the sea. Mankind was still young, and built its empires along the disregarded coasts. With the sea safely at their backs, the defenses of men faced inland, toward the enemies they most feared.

But man's greatest enemy has always been man.

Although he lived near the mouth of the Kohe'Tu river, Tar of Yunkai had never seen a ship. There were two reasons for this. First, the waters at the river's mouth were studded with submerged rocks that gutted any hull larger than a fishing-boat. Second, the Yunkai were said to be demons. Some claimed they were born with fur and fangs. Others said they changed into wolves at night.

Tar had lived thirteen summers when the slave-hunters raided his village.

Three ships came from the south. Their captain, Scimi the Black, knew nothing about the region except that it was seldom harvested for men, and would be unprepared for an attack. Atlantis had an endless need for slaves. Because of this, long stretches of southern coast had been stripped of their populations. Only in hard-to-reach places could human prey still be found—such as the Kohe'Tu river.

Scimi stroked the fierce black beard that gave him his name. He was legendary for his skill at navigating dangerous waters. He could read currents like a map.

He guided his three long, low ships through the shoals of submerged rocks by watching the pattern of the swirling water. His pathfinding was impeccable. He steered his fleet up the river, and soon saw the reed-walled Yunkai huts along the high ground.

The ships came hissing through the river current and drove their prows upon the white beach. Their figureheads arched like snakes about to strike. Before the oars were up, forty men sprang from the decks and charged the quiet village.

The slavers were pirates by trade. They carried torches, cutlasses, and three-pointed spears. As they rushed toward the huts, naked brown folk ducked inside, or fled into the forest that fringed the waterfront.

This much was typical in such raids—the ships had raided another village the previous day, and its unfortunate inhabitants fled or hid just the same. But what happened next had never occurred before.

The pirates were halfway to the first hut when they were met with overwhelming force. Straight through their thatched walls leapt the villagers. Armed with well-kept steel, they fell on the invaders like tigers.

Roars of pirate bloodlust turned to screams of terror. Limbs flew spurting from their joints and guts were tangled in the sand. Within the first minute, a dozen of the pirates were dead. Yunkai men and women fought side by side, slashing the enemy with abandon. Their children would pop out of hiding places to slay the mortally wounded with flint knives, then conceal themselves again.

Although Tar's tribe lived by fishing, its heritage was war. The ancestral steel with which the villagers fought had been quenched a thousand times in blood. The first of his people had come from across the Eastern Sea, hewing their way through a hundred nations, and settled in this place only because their numbers were too few to continue on, and their enemies too numerous to go back. A hundred years and more they had lived there, tending their fighting traditions like a sacred flame.

Scimi had heard vague tales of such a tribe, but didn't believe them. Now he did. He had never seen common people so eager to fight.

The crews of the first two ships were massacred among the huts. Bloodied survivors fled to the third ship. Some made it aboard, but not all. Fearing a counter-attack, the intact crew thrust their vessel back into the waves.

The pirates wanted easy kills and ready plunder. They were only courageous when victory was certain. Opposed, they fled to raid another day. Scimi was no different. He bellowed the commands that set the oars to flee. He saw the men he'd abandoned fall to the crimson blades of the Yunkai. The river was stained red.

The Yunkai were not done. From the treeline swarmed arrows. They were drilled with holes to make them scream as they came down, studding the naked backs of oar-slaves and pirates alike. Half of Scimi's crew were clawing at the barbs that pierced their bodies before the ship was out of range. Scimi could hear the villagers laughing as they loosed their bows—it was sport for them.

Only one of the raiders had caught himself a prize.

A boy, twelve or thirteen years of age, was slung over his shoulder. He hadn't captured the child for a slave, but used him as a living shield to escape the village.

Scimi ordered the snake-headed prow of his remaining

ship turned to the open horizon. The sails filled and what oars remained tore at the water.

"What devils were those?" Scimi demanded of the gods. "I have sailed every coast south of here, and never encountered such fighting savages!"

"I'd heard tales, but thought them nonsense dreamed up by cowards," said First Mate Skraj. "I feared the pithecines more, until today. Are they demons?"

Skraj's bald scalp was split to the bone by a sword-cut, so that his skull peeped through like the white of an eye; the man didn't yet know the extremity of his wound, or he would have collapsed upon the deck.

"I captured one," said the sailor who had taken Tar. "If it's a demon, it's disguised as a boy."

Scimi ordered the child brought up to the foredeck that he might see what make of men they had encountered. He expected the child to have claws, at the very least.

The boy was unconscious. Scimi understood why he had not resisted capture like the rest of his kind—he'd been stabbed half a dozen times. The boy was muscular for his age, hard of limb, brown-skinned, with eyes the color of ripe grain. His black hair was tawny from the sun.

"Bind his wounds, and if he lives, I'll learn what sort of creature he is," Scimi said. "If we could capture a score of those people they would gain great fame in the arenas of Thohar, Kita, Magon, and even Atlantis herself, and their price would make us rich."

2

———————

Their forces greatly reduced, the slavers turned their prows homeward to Khatha. It was slow going with few able slaves at the oars. Fickle winds played hide-and-seek with the sails.

For the first week of the voyage, the boy was dying, his wounds hot, swollen, and weeping. The following week they shrank and went dry.

Scimi had never seen anyone survive such wounds, let alone a child. But when they first sluiced the blood from his limbs the pirates saw that the lad's flesh was already marked by old injuries, despite his youth.

Time and again he returned to the side of the grievously ill child and stood there brooding, his fingers winding corkscrews in his beard. If he resembled a worried parent, it was only an outward similarity. More than anything, he yearned to peel the boy's skin off and fly it like a flag on the masthead. But only the Gods could have placed such temptation before him—as bait to test his will. Scimi could not strike without risking the wrath of the Gods, and it drove him mad.

.   .   .

AFTER FIFTEEN WEARY DAYS, the slavers reached the marble-hewn port of Khatha. Two ships of the enterprise were gone, and the surviving ship's hold was nearly empty of slaves and goods. It was a cataclysmic humiliation.

Scimi would be the object of ridicule in the courts and markets of the city. His pride stung bitterly.

At the dock, he oversaw the unloading of the few slaves he had collected, and ordered the boy taken on a litter to his quarters in the sea captain's street of the city. Their captives from the less violent tribe would be fattened up for a few days, their injuries and sores healed or concealed. In this way they would fetch a higher price.

As for the boy, Scimi decided the treacherous Gods had indeed set him a trap, and that he should not hasten the child's departure from the world. Let *them* decide if he lived or not. Scimi had other things to worry about.

Three weeks from the day of his capture, the boy had still not regained consciousness. There was talk among the servants that Scimi wanted the child alive because he reminded him of his long-dead son. Others said he wanted to look him in the eyes before killing him.

Even the best doctors could not determine the cause of the boy's coma. It might have been exsanguination, or it might have been a witch-curse. The doctors thought Scimi was a fool to squander money and medicine on a useless captive, but as long as his gold held out, they'd let him squander it.

In fact it was gold that now kept Scimi fixated on the boy. He dreamed of capturing that entire village and selling its ferocious inhabitants at a fortune per head. Scimi would keep a few for himself—he could breed their speed, toughness, and discipline into Khatha's common slave bloodlines, which he thought decadent.

But to recoup his losses and outfit such a dangerous mission, he would first have to sell everything he owned—his palace, his lands, his slaves and shares, and even the boy. Before he did so, he needed to learn everything about the Yunkai in order to plan the raid, and that meant waking the damnable child up.

"MASTER, you spend wealth you do not possess."

Scimi snapped out of his brooding trance.

Klith-Oha was pouring peppered wine as he spoke. The captain's major-domo, Klith-Oha oversaw his master's finances. He dreaded to discuss the matter of money, but he had no choice. His smooth, plump skin was dappled with sweat.

The evening was warm, but cooler than the day, so they were outside on the front terrace. Scimi's private chamber was within, the boy's sickbed in an alcove there.

"That child will never recover his wits, Master. His body seems mostly healed. But his brain is lost. He hasn't spoken a word or opened his eyes. You know that sometimes great loss of blood steals the wits of a man. So it is with this boy. Eat his liver, make some good boots of his skin, and be done with it."

"The gods demand I keep him," Scimi muttered. He was beginning to think the whole voyage had been cursed, and was wondering which of his rivals had the resources to summon strong magic.

"The truth is, Captain...if he does not come back to himself in the next week, you will have to make a choice. There isn't treasure enough in the vaults for the best doctors to visit more than once again. Then we'll have to borrow money from the Shaha. If only the voyage had been more profitable..."

"Oh shut up," Scimi barked. "His people cost me almost everything. So he will make me rich. That is how the Gods work. Great advancement follows great trials. He is my trial, so my advancement also lies in him."

Tar was pleased to hear this.

He had been listening to the conversation, as he listened every night.

3

This night, Tar was crouched in a place of concealment inside the archway between bedchamber and terrace.

On nights when Scimi went to bed, Tar would also sleep. His palette was visible from Scimi's own silken couch, so he couldn't risk being absent.

Luckily, such nights were few. Mostly the pirate drank himself to sleep on the terrace, his tormented thoughts drugged to stillness by wine and balmy sea air and the knocking of waves upon the thousand hulls moored in the harbor below.

Klith-Oha never interrupted his master after he was drunk, so Tar could come and go unobserved as long as Scimi snored and drooled on his tablecloth.

After two hands of days, Tar had recovered enough to fight, which was his people's measure of good health. At that time the slavers were still far from Khatha. A day later, the ship stopped for water where the Gurun River spilled over a rocky escarpment and into the sea. The boy considered escaping there.

Tar, like all Yunkai, believed misfortune was a lesson delivered by the Gods. The closer one came to death, the greater the lesson to be learned. Unfortunately, despite hovering at the edge of destruction for so long, he had no idea what the lesson was.

He would discover it eventually—his misfortunes were not over yet. He was at least a month's walk from his village. He would have to cross plains of grass where the herds were stalked by knife-toothed lions. He would have to trek through forests dominated by flesh-eating pigs and bands of iron-limbed pithecines. Yunkai explained pithecines to their children with a saying: *Meet man, man meat.*

Tar was certain he would understand the lesson by the time his journey was over. So he must begin at once.

Yet even as he prepared to slip over the gunwale of the ship, the pirates all being occupied with getting of water and repairs to the sail, he hesitated.

His people were explorers by nature. This wanderlust had driven his ancestors thousands of miles from their ancient homeland. It occurred to him that if he visited Khatha and returned to tell tales of it, he might regain the honor he had lost by getting captured.

So Tar decided not to escape, and remained in his fever-bed aboard the ship for the entire voyage, feigning unconsciousness. It wasn't difficult. He was weak and his wounds were still painful. He was a child. Even the hardest of children takes comfort when he can.

"Don't let yourself grow soft," he muttered, flexing his muscles against themselves to keep his strength.

Since the arrival of the ship in Khatha, Tar had been busy in the deep of the nights. He had learned much. Scimi discussed the ill-fated voyage with his fellow captains. The pirate often drank with them on the terrace when the sun was down and the sky still purpled with the memory of the day. In this way, Tar learned he was the only Yunkai captured.

Tar also learned Scimi's weaknesses. Besides debt, he was prey to slave-girls with long black brows and heavy breasts. He was also prey to scented wine, superstition, opium incense, and greed.

Tar knew the major-domo's weakness as well.

On several occasions during days when Scimi was absent, Tar had felt Klith-Oha's soft hands exploring his body. He didn't stir, no matter where those creeping fingers went. But he felt burning shame. He wanted to kill the man.

After a week ashore, Tar couldn't lie still any longer. He resolved to explore the city, and so began his late-night forays. He soon knew the street of sea captains well. It commanded views far out over the ocean, which is why it was favored by these men.

He found several routes of escape from the city, including a weak place in the walls which surrounded it—an ancient temple where sacred fig trees grew, their roots dangling down on either side of the fortification, as good as a ladder. He discovered the stables where the tens of thousands of new slaves were chained up, ready for market. The stench of that place was beyond endurance.

He learned of the Khathian people, too. For some reason the Khathian men kept their women idle, and encouraged them to be helpless. This Tar had learned the night he reached the wealthy quarter of the town, where painted women were carried in palanquins by gleaming, oiled slaves. The richest women did nothing for themselves, and appeared almost to be puppets. The poorest offered their bodies to passing men as if they were selling fried grubs.

Strangest of all to him were the children. Even the wild beggar-children, who should have been tough and resilient, seemed broken in spirit. Why did they grovel for copper coins

and starve in the filth, when there was rich forest and grass-
land outside the city gates? Why did the wealthy children
play with dolls instead of knives?

He found the city and its people to be soft as melons.
They were heart-rotten. How could such a mighty land lack
any discipline? He believed his village could overthrow the
city.

Even the soldiers that guarded the hilltop palaces were a
shambles. It was deeply shameful to Tar that he had been
defeated by a pirate from this place. He consoled himself
with the thought that the man had been four times his size,
armed with a trident, and that two of his fellows had died in
the attempt.

That sailor and Scimi were on the list of people Tar
intended to kill. Major-domo Klith with his moist and
wandering fingers was at the top of the list.

Tar was content to play dead in the daytime and go out
secretly at night—until he overheard Klith telling Scimi the
money had run out. It was time to act.

4

———

The greatest enemy of all was boredom, and Tar was bored witless. There was much of the city he had not explored, for the distances he could go each night were limited—he must be back before the servants checked on him, and his feet must be clean as if he'd never stirred.

Lying in bed was torment, too. He'd never slept so much, and he felt his muscles softening despite his efforts. He determined to escape that same night Klith-Oha delivered his warning. He'd go crazy otherwise.

Tar might have slipped out of the city and been gone forever from Scimi's small circle of influence, except he decided to exact a quick revenge on Klith-Oha before he left. The man slept in a ground floor room beneath Scimi's own chamber. There was a small garden outside his door, for he was housed on the inland side of the building. Tar scaled down the bronze roof drain and alighted silently in the garden. He saw the major-domo inside his chamber, kneeling in prayer before an altar on the wall in which stood a golden figure with a boar's head and many arms.

He went in—the doors were not locked—and took up a shaving razor. He was still young enough that stealthy killing was acceptable. The Yunkai were practical-minded about such things. So he slit the major-domo's throat from behind.

Klith spewed blood from his nose and mouth, his fingers fondling the wound that half-severed his head. Then he slumped sideways and died on the floor. Tar kept the razor, tucking it into his breeches.

Bad luck came immediately. The pirate Scimi rang his silver summoning-bell. The major-domo would be expected to appear on his doorstep within moments.

Thinking quickly, Tar knocked over the tripod lamp that lit the room, and watched with satisfaction as the oil soaked into the major-domo's robes and bedclothes. The flames followed eagerly. Tar went out into the garden and over the wall, and was ten houses away when he heard the first shouts of alarm.

It was then he learned something else about city guards— they would capture anyone running from the scene of a fire. He ran straight into the arms of a patrol, and failed to do what a city-bred boy would do: He fought when he should have cowered. They might have lacked discipline, but the soldiers were tough, and much larger, and Tar was swiftly immobilized, only cutting two men with the razor before he was overcome.

WHEN SCIMI DISCOVERED what had happened, he was enraged. To be tricked by a boy, his house burned, and his favorite servant murdered! The man would have slain Tar the moment he learned the news, but once the boy was captured by the crown guards, he became property of Khatha's king, Ygr-On.

Scimi couldn't touch him. So he devised a worse fate.

Slavers were favored by King Ygr-On. They brought great wealth and useful human material for empire-building. Scimi begged the king for an audience. The king said he would listen. Scimi begged to be allowed to take the hateful child to Atlantis itself.

Scimi had to go there no matter what: the fire had ruined his palace. He couldn't finance his planned raid on the Yunkai. He would have to humble himself and spend the next year running errands to Atlantis. His surviving ship was swift but light. It would be used to carry slaves, diplomats, and letters in a hurry, rather than wine, metals, and earth, as the bigger ships did.

The king agreed to let Scimi take the boy to Atlantis on two conditions: First, that the boy arrive alive and capable; and second, that he give the boy as tribute to Harpan of House Wetè, the king of Atlantis.

So began Tar's descent into slavery.

KHATHA'S ARENA was the third-largest in the known world, the greatest being the royal fighting-pit in Atlantis. The arena at Khatha boasted, in addition to mock slave raids and thousand-sword mêlées, a broad program of tortures. They made criminals, dissidents, and slaves suffer there, and it was considered fine sport.

Scimi had been attending torture shows since he was Tar's age, and had seen hundreds of techniques for wringing prolonged agony from the human frame. He knew a good deal about what would kill and maim, and what would only break the will. He had also practiced these arts on his captives, when he thought they were hiding treasure from him, or some other secrets, or if he was bored.

To occupy the two weeks' voyage to Atlantis, Scimi refined his torturer's art. Every day he half-drowned the boy at least once, then hung him by his ankles to drain his lungs. Sometimes he hung him from a yardarm a few inches above the water, so that large waves would crash over the child, battering him senseless.

On other days he would lash hunks of raw fish to the boy and trail him in the water like bait, attracting the immense triple-finned sharks that hunted those parts; sailors would pull the boy back onto the vessel only when the fish were snapping at his heels with their fang-crowded jaws. The fins of these sharks were so tall they rose above the deck, so this was risky sport even for the sailors.

Atlantis was in mid-ocean then. Later in the year it would be close enough for coastal boats to visit it, and later still it would be out of range of all but the largest ships. Scimi wasted none of the voyage. When the boy wasn't tormented in the water, he got the worst of the weather on deck.

Thirst was his cruelest enemy, and he could not drink the sea. Scimi gave Tar small rations of fresh water to keep him alive, but no more. Then the boy might be strapped to the deck to suffer the heat of noontime, or to freeze at night, his limbs pulled so taut he could barely even shiver.

There were other tortures, too – things Scimi allowed his brutal sailors to do, amusements they might otherwise have paid for in the whore's quarter of Atlantis. They committed outrages on his body that the major-domo Klith would not have dared to consider.

One after another they tormented the boy, until all assumed his spirit was broken. He was nearly silent in any case, but after a week of this torture he uttered not a sound. The once-proud head that was raised defiantly to all now began to hang, and his eyes were downcast. The boy never struggled or fought any more.

Scimi was glad. He had been tricked and shamed by this adolescent demon. Now that the boy was destroyed in mind and racked in body, he could begin to enjoy himself again, and forget how ridiculous he had been made back in Khatha.

In this way, the pirate made the same mistake as before, for Tar was tricking him in the same way. Tar was not spirit-broken, but only pretending, in the same manner he had pretended to be sick from his wounds. Every horror he endured, every misery, only strengthened his will. Wasn't red-hot steel tempered by the shock of icy water? Suffering endured becomes strength.

The only thing that changed, from Tar's perspective, was that he had a much longer list of people to kill.

His hatred he threw into deep pits in his soul. With every fresh cruelty he thought the pits must fill up, but they only became deeper. Later in his life that hatred would become a source of energy, an inexhaustible mine to fuel his ambitions.

Three days from Atlantis, the torture ended. Scimi had the wretched youth fed, and herbed fat was smeared on his sores. The sailors were forbidden from abusing him any further. Scimi had no intention of giving the boy to the king of Atlantis, despite his promise. A slave so promising was worth too much gold, which Scimi badly needed since the disastrous raid. He would sell the boy instead.

ON THE FINAL day of the voyage, Tar saw Atlantis for the first time.

5

———

The first sight of the floating island, which Tar glimpsed from a wooden cage on the deck, was of a glittering golden line between sea and sky, stretching across half the horizon. The once-lonely waves became crowded. There were many ships heading to and from Atlantis, their canvas cracking in the wind. Small fishing boats circled the island like minnows, their sails mere flecks in the shadows of the vast pontoons.

Legends of the landborn folk said Atlantis was a thousand miles in diameter. It was closer to twenty-five. Some said it rode on the backs of tamed leviathans from the time before walking beasts. In truth, Atlantis floated on tens of thousands of mighty bronze pontoons, the largest of which displaced nearly a million tons of water each. They were fashioned to look like giant sea-monsters, which gave rise to the legend. Atlantis was not a continent of stone and earth like the other three of the world, but an island floating on the surface of the sea.

As the ship drew closer, Tar saw details emerge along the shining horizon. There was a forest of immense masts that rose up in the center of the island, each mast supporting dozens of huge sails, every sail bearing the heraldic device of some great house. There were also masts naked of sails from which descended webs of chain and cable, which must have been braces to keep everything level and true. Tall towers and broad palaces punctuated the skyline, some green with age, some shining like fire. There were spires and domes of copper, bronze, gold, and silver. Flags and pennants the size of wheat fields flew from many a rooftop, silks snapping and furling in the constant breeze.

Despite his dark mood and bleak future, Tar admired the view. It was awesome, and had he not come to that place to die, it would have lifted his spirits to see a wonder so famous with his own eyes.

Now the pontoons towered up above his cage, their vast sea-greened faces scowling down through a blizzard of white gulls, and there were glimpses of busy harbors among them.

Scimi shouted orders, the sail came down, long oars plunged into the water, and and the oar-master began to beat time on his kelenken-skin drum. Groaning, whip-shy slaves rowed the vessel into one of the countless inlets that fringed the periphery of Atlantis.

They sculled past dry-docks in which hung mighty ships, and artificial bays crowded with every manner of craft. The air was noisy with shouts of men and seabirds and the gurgle and rush of the waves as they sloshed between the immense bronze floats that bore Atlantis up. The street-level deck was eighty feet above the water. Tar could see little of it, except glimpses of shops and houses made of metal.

Scimi's ship passed alongside an enormous green-skinned pipe from which belched reeking sewage drained from the streets above. Tar could not believe so much filth existed in all the world.

He saw now that there were gangs of ragged men and

women chained to swaying catwalks that were suspended between the floats. These wretched souls labored in fetid blue-green darkness. He watched them.

Some hammered plates over holes in the pontoon's skins, and others mopped grease onto cyclopean chains with links the size of elephants. Even as Tar looked on, a slave woman was crushed in the joint of two of these links. She burst apart like an insect and her entrails spilled into the mouths of eager fish in the sea below. The other slaves chained to her few remains continued working as if nothing had happened.

"That's to be you, if my client won't have you," Scimi remarked, echoing Tar's thoughts. He had been watching the youth's face to see his reaction to Atlantis. The pirate gloated:

"This voyage was a pleasure-cruise compared to that. I wish I could watch you die. But only the gods receive complete satisfaction, for they witness all."

Tar had never heard that before. He would have to remember it. It might be that his own vengeance would be wrought in ways he couldn't see; he must be content in that case. Captain Scimi, however, he intended to see die—and at very close range.

THE SLAVES RAISED oars and the graceful, snake-headed ship glided into its berth among the hundreds of others moored alongside the quays of Atlantis. Ropes were thrown and orders shouted, and the ship was secured in its place.

An official in a tall, embroidered mitre cap met Scimi on the deck, and counted off the few slaves as they were whipped up from the hold and hurried along the gangplank to a prison under the dock. Two pirates carried Tar's cage up to the dockside level above these slaves, where strange animals and birds were also chained up. It stank, but Tar preferred the stench of animals to humans. Over everything lay powerful sea smells, of fish and brine and kelp.

For two hours Tar crouched in his cage. He heard cries of fear and anguish from below as the other slaves were separated into categories for sale. Then huge-armed men with rags knotted around their brows came to his level. They led some animals on ropes and bore away others in their cages. Eventually Tar was the only creature left.

Scimi returned, in company with the fattest man Tar had ever seen. He was nearly spherical. He wore sleeves of cloth of gold worked with red gems. His naked bosom was as ample as a woman's backside. His head was shaven smooth and speckled with droplets of sweat.

"This is the one," Scimi said. "He killed a dozen of my men in combat before he succumbed to his wounds. I nursed him back to health, and here he is. He's savage, of course. Not a drop of civilized blood in his veins. But then, that's what the fighting-pit needs."

The heavy man circled Tar's cage. He stroked his uppermost chin. The man smelled strange—a sickly-sweet, rotten stink overlaid with strong perfume.

"A dozen of your men? He's only a stripling."

The heavy fellow was no fool, thought Tar. He didn't know exactly how many a dozen was, but it was more than his fingers. He'd only killed both thumbs of men, not both hands of men.

"I'll give you five gold serpents for him," the heavy man said.

"Five? He's worth five hundred full-grown!"

"But he's small now, and to raise him to adulthood would cost me ten thousand. These fighters eat like bears. Anyway there's a new sport in the arena – we put a few dozen children in there with all sorts of light weapons and the ones who kill one of their playmates are allowed to live. Those who will not fight are fed to the spiders. It's very fair. We group them by age, and only six summers and up. The younger ones won't do it."

"I must see this while I'm here," Scimi said, admiration in his voice.

"There's one every half-moonday," the heavy man said. "How old is this lad?"

"Sixteen," Scimi said. He knew better, of course—Tar couldn't possibly be that age. But he wanted the boy fighting bigger opponents.

"He doesn't look a day over fourteen, but if he's as formidable as you say, I'll put that down. Seven serpents, isn't that what we agreed?"

Scimi was not pleased, but he took the money. Four slaves with plumed headdresses picked up the cage and bore Tar away. Seven serpents was the price of a camel.

6

On the journey to the arena, Tar saw more of Atlantis. For what seemed an eternity, he was carried through the stinking, dappled shadows of the under-decks. A tremendous noise, sharpened by the metal surfaces all around, pierced his ears. Everyone was shouting and bashing. In a decade, the entire Yunkai tribe didn't make as much noise as any laborer here could make in a single minute. Eventually the slaves bore him up a clanging ramp to street level, where the sun shone down on a dazzling scene.

His experiences in Khatha had been limited to late-night roaming like an alley cat, when few people were out, and the houses and shops were shut. Only the pleasure streets had been busy then. He'd never seen another city, so that is how he understood them to be.

Now he saw the mightiest city in the world at its busiest hour. His bearers brought him up into one of the market quarters. All was color, noise, bustle and stench.

There were thousands of people on every side, naked-breasted, jostling and arguing and shouting their wares. They came from every race and nation. Rich silks mingled with rotten rags, polished armor, and veils of sheerest gossamer. There were black, brown, red, and tawny faces. Some were men, some were pithecines, and others Tar knew not.

Anything in the world was available in the shops and stalls—vegetables, meat, fish, rich and common cloth, iron, bronze, copper, silver and gold, tables and chairs, boats and palanquins, beasts of every kind—everything that could be wrought, mined, woven, or grown could be had at a price.

They passed through a street devoted exclusively to the sale of colorful exotic birds, which shrieked and preened or slept with heads tucked under their wings, in cages and on stands. There were birds in pens as tall as two men that glared down defiantly at the crowds, snapping their heavy razor-edged beaks.

Tar wondered how he could escape his cage. There were endless places to hide in these streets. He tested the locks and tugged on every bar. There was no getting out.

The slaves turned left and jostled the cage along a way that captivated Tar, for it suited his mood: The street of armorers. Each stall was laden with gleaming implements of death, many of which he recognized, but there were others which suggested possibilities for violence he'd never considered before— poisoned hair-pins, gloves with sharp talons, spears with tips that spread out like flowers on impact, and countless more refinements to bring death to an enemy.

This street ended in the shadow of a huge, oval structure, clad in bronze chased with gold, and crowned with fluttering banners. Its walls were carved with scenes of combat. Into this building Tar was carried by the slaves, marching down echoing passages until they came to a broad door fashioned from whale bones.

The heavy man descended from the palanquin in which he had been carried by six slaves, and spoke to the scale-mailed guards there. They bowed and opened the door. Tar's cage was carried through into a bright sunlit courtyard with very tall copper sides, like an enormous bucket. A familiar sound met his ears: steel clashing with steel.

"Open it," the heavy man said, and a slave released the locks on Tar's cage. The boy crawled stiffly out, all his attention on the scene before him. Two young men were fighting with blunt swords on the crushed-shell floor of the space, cutting and stabbing and sometimes grappling. Onlookers shouted encouragement.

Most of them were naked except for *pteruges*, skirts made of long leather strips. The fighters were agile and strong, and very determined. A dozen others waited their turns. Trainers bellowed advice. Guards leaned on lances, watching. Tar also watched, feeling the numbness leave his cramped limbs. A cracking blow across one fighter's skull ended the bout, and the combatants were separated.

The heavy man came close, and the sweet stink of rotten fruit filled Tar's nostrils.

"I am Heptumu, master of pit-slaves," said the man. "I train the best in Atlantis. I also train the best foils, which are folk who have just enough skill to defend themselves and keep things interesting, but don't stand a fart's chance in a hurricane of winning."

He seemed to expect Tar to reply, but the boy had nothing to say, so he didn't. Heptumu, however, was always happy to speak, even to a worthless child he'd soon send to die.

"There are scores of arenas all around the city, but this one, the Crimson Arena, is the most prestigious. Isn't that flattering? You've been bought by the best—me. Now let's see if you're a fighter or a foil. Seven gold serpents—gods help me, at least survive this test."

Heptumu clapped his hands. A sweating trainer in loin-cloth and leather shin-greaves threw a thick iron sword at

Tar's feet. Tar picked it up. It weighed as much as his own leg. The trainer blew a whistle made from a fish vertebra.

From the crowd of fighters came a grinning man of eighteen or nineteen whose nose had been cut off, so that his breath hissed through tall red slits. This man carried a bone-shafted spear with a blunt metal tip. His right side was armored with sharkskin.

Tar could barely feel his limbs—the cage was very small and he'd been in it for hours. The fighter was two feet taller than him, and weighed much more. But he'd lost his nose, so he wasn't invincible. Tar observed that he always kept his armored side forward. As well, the shaft of the spear was notched from long use, weaker than it looked. Simple enough. Tar threw the iron sword aside and crouched low, and waited for the first thrust of the spear.

"Seven gold serpents," Heptumu groaned.

I⊤ WAS over in a few swift moves. The grinning noseless man came in hard and overconfident, and thrust the spear. Tar twisted and dropped his weight on the shaft, which bent and splintered. He rolled, and came up behind, on his opponent's unarmored side. The broken butt-end of the spear was in his hands.

As the noseless man turned, Tar jammed the jagged end of the spear into the exposed joint between thigh and groin. Blood spewed out in a fan. The man roared with pain and danced nimbly away, getting his armored side back around. Tar waited. For several seconds his opponent didn't realize the fight was already over.

Then loss of blood set in, he swayed and fell, and his heart emptied his veins as he struggled weakly in the sand.

"He's not a foil," said the trainer in leather greaves, and shouted with laughter.

"The dead man cost me *fifteen* serpents," Heptumu complained.

But Tar saw that the heavy man was impressed, because he'd stepped behind a pair of guards with proper armor and weapons. Heptumu stood there fiddling with his gaudy finger-rings, and looked well pleased.

Tar scanned the faces around him as a laugh went up among the fighters—he saw two that were not laughing, fighters the same age as the man lying dead in the sand. They must have been comrades. He'd have to watch them. Then the trainer clapped a hard paw on Tar's shoulder, plucking the bloody shaft of bone from his grasp.

"First piece of advice: save the killing for the main arena. Second piece of advice: go bathe. You stink enough to kill a wild pig, and I think you know how they smell, based on the way you took down Indiro there. That was a forest hunter's move. There's a trough with soap and water through that gateway. They'll fit you up with a fresh set of pteruges as well. Come back in half an hour and we'll get started."

So it was that Tar began life as a pit-fighter.

7

Every day he trained and fought, and his childhood became ever-more distant. The early matches were with boys his own age, and the fights sickened him. He had observed in Khath how city children seemed helpless and soft, even the rough street urchins. It was as if they didn't think life had begun, or could ever end. Each time he was sent into the huge main ring with its stands full of cheering crowds and scowling gilt-bronze statues, he felt as if he were slaughtering kittens.

He saw what happened to those who refused to fight—the gladiators could view the action through grilles set into the foot of the walls, while waiting their own turns on the sand.

The children who lay down and covered their heads, or ran away to cower behind columns, were left in the arena as their slain and wounded companions were thrown into carts and taken away. Then savage animals would be released from four gates set equidistant around the ring.

Once all the cowardly children were torn apart, the next entertainment would begin. Tar was not going to die that way. So he killed boys and girls his own age and older, trying to make it swift, not looking into their terrified faces.

He was far too angry and bitter for one so young. The only thing that sustained him was the chance to improve his skills through training. If he must spend his days spattered with the blood of weaklings, he was going to use those days to become strong enough to slay those who were not weak.

He was soon placed in matches with young men like the one he'd killed that first day – between sixteen and eighteen years of age. Those were harder fights. He was often wounded, but never lost. None who returned to the arena had lost a fight—mercy was unknown in Atlantis' pits.

Eventually he faced both of the men who had been friends of Indiro, the noseless man. He killed them. Their desire for revenge against one of their own kind seemed stupid to him. They were in the pits to die. It didn't matter who killed whom.

He learned to fight with long and short hand weapons, throwing weapons, blunt weapons, and chain weapons. He trained to kill with his feet and hands, then his knees and elbows. He learned the anatomy of the human body, and all of the ways to destroy it.

He was taught the strengths and weaknesses of armor, and which metals were best for every purpose. The fighters hated Atlantean steel, for example. It did not rust, and remained bright as silver. But it was brittle, and often shattered when struck. Everyone loved iron, at once hard and malleable, but it was heavy and could not endure the sea air of Atlantis. They all had opinions about the toughest leather, the best weight of spear, and the quickest way to kill.

Before every fight, the fighting slaves would clasp each other's wrists and recite the pit-fighter's goodbye:

"Die with a red blade."

And so they did. But Tar lived on.

For three years, he endured. His balls dropped, his voice grew deeper, and his face and back were speckled with pimples. These things would have consumed the attention of an ordinary youth. Tar cared for nothing but his increasing strength and skill. He kept himself apart in the dormitories, at meals, and on the days when they were free to rest.

Most fighters Tar's age would play pranks on each other, sword-fight with their erections, and have competitions for who could squeeze out the most prodigious blackhead. They found ways to be teenaged fools despite the deadly nature of their occupation. Tar, however, could never forget what he was there to do. He knew his peers were right when they accused him of lacking a sense of humor, but they kept dying and he kept living.

Sometimes he wondered what his people at home thought of him. He'd been wounded and captured, which was a dishonor unheard-of among the Yunkai. They probably thought he was dead, if they thought of him at all. Life would go on. He pictured the small plots of fruit trees they'd planted in the jungle, and the places where they would dig for edible roots. He remembered long days on the river, or out in the ocean, fishing with his father and his uncles. He remembered humid nights waiting for the giant boars to crash past their blind and furnish the tribe with roasted meat that ran with molten fat. He remembered the band of wary pithecines whose territory ran up against the Yunkai's— sometimes friends, sometimes foes, according to the logic of that race.

Was his elder sister still the best with a short bow in all the tribe? What were his other siblings doing? He had a brother and two sisters. His brother had a stump for an arm. The tribe was tolerant of the infirm, but not helpful. A Yunkai with one arm must make up the difference by himself. Did he still live?

Tar's memories of home were fading. After his years in the pits, he couldn't clearly picture his mother's face, or remember how tall his father was. His past was becoming hard to conjure up, as if it were buried in the ground-up shells that paved the arena. It didn't matter. Only the present was important. Only the fight to survive.

8

———

Unlike Tar, Heptumu had his eyes on the future.

He was a talented showman, and wanted to dominate his profession. As soon as Tar revealed fighting promise, he'd fitted the boy with a beautiful silver mask in the likeness of a god, with a helmet cunningly wrought to look like golden hair.

There was a slave whose job it was to polish the weapons and armor. This slave shined the mask and helm after every fight to keep it flashing. Tar's face, however, nobody saw outside the slave quarters. The public came to know him as the Golden Youth. Other fighters called him the Yellow Cobra, because of this lethal striking speed.

Tar grew to be neither large nor small. The clay-painted giants from the south were taller than he could reach up with his arms. Dwargs, who were thick of limb, great of strength, and could crush a man's skull in their hands, were shorter than him—but twice as broad. He fought them and won.

Some of his foes were of no race he could identify. There were lion-colored folk with blue-stained backs, and people whose skins were striped and spotted. Once he fought a tattooed, orange-haired man from the far northwest, with skin as pale as bone and eyes the color of the sky. The man was uncommonly fierce and seemed to feel no pain, but died just the same.

As he grew, Tar had to adjust his fighting technique. The upward stabs and groin slashes no longer suited his height, but now he could hack downward and grapple full-grown men.

Although anonymous, he became famous as the Golden Youth. Heptumu moved him to a private cell, away from the dormitories.

Tar often received fawning letters and gifts from admirers. The letters he could not read, nor could his guards. They were all illiterate. Heptumu read them all, looking for potential blackmail and gossip. He would quote the more amusing ones for Tar during his weekly visits to the slave quarters. His sweet stink seemed to poison the fawning words.

The gifts sent to the Golden Prince were often of enormous value, imported from distant lands—flowers, wine, fruits, nuts, jewelry and silks. Heptumu kept the metals and jewels. Tar shared the food and drink generously with his guards. Relaxed and friendly watchmen could be of considerable advantage if the right opportunity arose.

The guards began to allow him visits to the flat roof of the slave quarters, where he could bask in the sun and exercise alone. The guards would lounge by the roof hatch and play dice or fishbones, equally glad to be out of the dank, perpetually chilly barracks.

ONE EVENING, when Tar was sixteen summers of age, Heptumu came to the slave quarters and informed him that he'd survived three entire years in the arena. That made Tar the fifth-longest survival in the history of the Atlantean pits.

Six more moons and he would be granted his freedom, in accordance with Atlantean law. He was now to be known as the Golden Prince.

Heptumu held a jug of good wine in his heavily-ringed hands. He poured them each a draught. Tar buried his nose in his cup to block out Heptumu's strange odor.

"To your success, my Golden Prince. It's only a pity," the heavy man mused, "that you're so thoroughly unbeatable. You move faster than the eye can follow. You have the strength of a man twice your size. Are all your people this good?"

"I'm the least of them—none of the others got captured."

"Astonishing. Where *do* you come from?"

Tar had learned from experience that Heptumu was at his most dangerous when he was at his friendliest. This casual question, posed as if a mere pleasantry over wine, was nothing of the sort. Tar didn't know what lay behind it, but he knew it wouldn't be good. Nonetheless, he did not lie:

"We come from the Kohe'Tu river that flows from the breast of Mother Anvil. My village is near the mouth of it, on the southern bank where the waters mingle."

"Fascinating," Heptumu said, in a tone that meant the opposite. But Tar saw the big man had begun to perspire, his rotten odor becoming more intense. He was excited about something, compulsively twisting the rings on his thick fingers.

Tar had spoken the truth about his village. It was of no use to Heptumu. To keep their hunting and fishing plentiful, the Yunkai moved up and down the river every year, building new huts wherever they settled. They would leave the old huts where they stood, to rot away from disuse. Should Heptumu arrange a slave-catching mission, his ships would find the village where Tar said—but not the Yunkai. The

Yunkai, however, would surely find his ships, and kill every man aboard.

Heptumu was lingering on this visit, and Tar wondered why. The man wasn't interested in his company, only his prowess as a fighter. At last he came to the point.

"In honor of your success," he said, pouring another cup, "I have bought you a woman. An underslave. She's yours until you die—may Iri-Tu-Ko, the god of money, forbid. You may not own property, of course, being a slave yourself. But I give you exclusive rights to her use, and she's yours when you retire."

Tar did not know what to say, so he busied himself draining the cup.

"You're welcome," Heptumu said. "I must see you taught some social graces. With freedom comes citizenship of Atlantis. You'll need to learn how one behaves in polite society. This isn't the jungle."

IN THE EVENING, the underslave was led into Tar's cell by one of the guards. The door locked behind her. She stood there in his simple room. She did not move, but her shadow shivered as if with fear in the light of the whale-oil lamp. Tar examined her as he would any opponent in the ring. He knew of no other way to look at people. She was afraid, but held her chin up, and stared back at him with all the courage she possessed. After a time, he spoke.

"What use is an underslave?"

"I will wash you, fuck you, and tend to your wounds, Golden Prince," she said.

"That's not much of a life. Who are you?"

"I am Motia, Golden Prince," she said.

"*That* is the Golden Prince," he said, gesturing at the

gleaming helmet of silver and gold that hung by the door. "My name is Tar Yunkai of Men."

"Tar," she repeated.

She knelt in submission, as slaves were expected to do when introduced to their new masters.

He continued examining her, and let the silence between them grow long. She was soft but not weak. Her skin was very dark, as if soaked in color. Even the whites of her eyes were flecked with brown. Although she was not big-breasted or fat-arsed, her proportions were pleasing to look at.

Tar knew a well-favored woman like her would never have been given to such a low scoundrel as him, except her face was scarred with the sun-symbol. That meant she was from the western shore of Tar's own continent, as he was from the east. Atlantis's dominant religion forbade deliberate alteration of the body, it being a holy vessel. Anyone with tattoos, brands, or ritual scarification was considered unclean. He didn't care. He had far more scars than her.

"Why do you not return my gaze?" He asked. She was staring at the floor.

"You have the yellow eyes of a lion."

"All my people do. It's only a color. I'm not half-beast as the rumors claim."

"I hope I please you," she whispered.

The tone of her voice did not match the words. She sounded to Tar as if she wanted to die.

He tried to smile, but those muscles in his face were rusty from disuse.

"Have you eaten? There is rich food in that basket. It is yours as you wish," he said. "I sleep on the floor in the manner of my people, so the bed is yours as well. I will not fuck you if you do not desire it. These civilized folk treat women like lesser creatures than men, but that is not the way of my people. Now I must sleep, for I spill more blood tomorrow. Snuff the lamp before you rest."

Tar took off his pteruges and boots, and lay down naked in the straw as was his custom. He composed his mind for sleep, ignoring the faint rustling as Motia began to move about the room. Then she spoke.

"Do you not desire me? My face is ugly but my body is good, and I am skilled at lovemaking."

He opened his eyes. She was standing naked, her tunic neatly folded on the bed. She had unclasped her hair. He looked at her high, big-nippled breasts and the black triangle between her thighs.

In truth, he fiercely desired her. But his voyage to Atlantis had been marked by ceaseless rape and violation. He would not inflict that torture on another. "I am as hard as an axe-handle," he admitted. "But you are afraid of me, so I will not touch you. Sleep in peace."

9

———————

He nearly lost his fight the next day—his testicles ached fiercely and distracted him, and he caught a hard blow from a spiked club, to the horror of the crowd. He was their favorite. But his opponent thought drawing blood was much the same as winning, and got cocky, and Tar eventually strangled the man with his own entrails.

He often went to sleep with such erections that he couldn't roll over. He would wake in the night and see Motia asleep on the bed, and watch the mood of her dreams. Sometimes she would frown, other times smile, and once she wept. But she never woke from these dreams, and Tar didn't ask her if she remembered them.

How she spent her days, he did not know. She had taken over polishing his armor. She prepared his simple meals, and accompanied him to the roof. While he exercised there, she would sit in the sun and watch the ocean roll beneath mighty Atlantis, gulls wheeling in the sky. They spoke a little in the evenings, but she was shy and downcast by nature, and he had little conversation in him.

As an underslave, Motia was permitted to do nothing but

what she was told. The trouble was that Tar needed nothing, or could do it himself. One thing he never had to endure was tedium. He felt he should invent tasks for her, just to keep her from going mad. He was responsible for her. He'd never been in such a position before. It was irritating, but he did not blame her.

Having responsibility for another person changed the combats for Tar: It made them even more dangerous. He began to suspect that this was the very reason he'd been given Motia. A fighter who appeared invincible was of little entertainment value, any more than a fighter guaranteed to die. There must be doubt, or people wouldn't place large bets.

As she grew more comfortable around him, Motia had begun to offer him small kindnesses. She might smile just to see him, or arrange an admirer's gift of flowers in a bowl to please his eye. When she closed his wounds with fish-gut thread, she was gentle, and asked if it pained him too greatly. Tar did not love her, but he found that he valued the companionship. The pit fighter's life was a lonely one. Even as a small boy, love was scarce. To cultivate hardness in their children, the Yunkai withdrew affection early. They preferred to reward accomplishments, not to make displays of fondness for no reason.

He discovered he was less worried for his own safety than hers. As a valuable slave, he had some privileges, but no rights. She had neither. If one of the guards decided to rape her, what could Tar do? Killing the man would be easy, but he would be slaughtered by the full force of Heptumu's garrison for it.

After a month together, he had still not taken her body. He wanted her, but would wait until she revealed if she truly desired him. The trouble was, she had been a slave since she was a small child, her facial scars barely healed.

She hid her own needs too well for him to guess what she wanted.

When lust tested his will, Tar would sometimes visit the sex-slaves Heptumu brought in each week. There were one or two who didn't hate the task. More often, he would take out his frustration on his opponents in the pits. This delighted the crowds, if not the men he butchered.

Heptumu began sending Tar to a small room full of books, where he received lessons on comportment and manners in Atlantis. He had never seen a library before. The books were strange objects. He examined them curiously. They contained thin golden sheets scribed with marks like the legs of insects, bound between boards wrapped in human skin. The overseer had told him the marks turned into thoughts if one knew the mystery of them. Tar did not believe this for an instant.

Once every week, the guards would shackle his foot to an Atlantean steel ring in the wall of the library. Eventually a thin, robed man with a nimbus of white hair would come in, coughing politely before he entered. He was by far the oldest person Tar had ever met.

This was Eregin Nimble of Men. He had been a dance instructor until he went lame with age, and knew all the manners of the court and good society. He had outlived two kings. He had endless stories of the great houses of Atlantis with which to illustrate his lessons, and was easily drawn into discussing topics not in the curriculum.

Tar found the old man fascinating. He was wise in the ways of the world and life in general, not only Atlantis. He was not at all afraid of Tar, and when they first met, objected to the shackle, but Heptumu didn't want to risk such a dangerous slave escaping into his private quarters, of which the library was a part.

"I am told you have an underslave," Eregin said during a lesson about the social castes of Atlantis.

"I do. Her name is Motia."

"Atlanteans do not volunteer the names of their slaves," Eregin corrected.

"I am not Atlantean."

"You will be, if you live another four moons. Some people last far longer than they anticipated—even fighters such as you. That is why I give lessons in comportment, you see. I need the money, having outlived my own savings by a considerable number of years."

"But why do you ask of my woman?"

"A slave with an underslave is in a different cast from his fellows. You came here as a beast—no more than a gazelle or pheasant. That is the lowest caste, the Dugra, which in the old tongue means 'meat'—because Dugra can be eaten. When you were bought by your master, you ascended to the next class, the Kogra—slaves. Of the same status is the Keedra, such as the white-skinned ones, pithecines, dwargs and imps. But Keedra are not necessarily slaves. Slaves with underslaves, such as yourself, are of the caste Adigra. If you survive to the end of your career in the fighting pits, you enter the Adigra-Kabra, lowest class of freemen."

"A freeman is a free man, be he fisherman or king. What higher caste is needed?"

"Young Tar, there is so much to teach you," said Eregin, and sipped spiny-urchin tea to ease his throat. At its strongest, his voice was hardly a whisper. "There are twelve castes. Do you know that number?"

"I cannot read or write, nor count," Tar said.

"Of course. I forget you are a landsman from the forests, and slaves are not taught these things. Twelve is both hands, plus both thumbs of another."

Tar counted this out with his own hands.

"That is many."

"It is, and it gets far more difficult to rise with every caste.

I am Paridra, fourth from the top. Four is one hand, no thumb. It took me sixty summers to get this far, and that by marriage and royal decree. To reach Uttaboraa, the highest caste, you must be born or adopted into it. Even marriage will not suffice—although the Uttaboraa only marry each other, so it's practically impossible to achieve."

Tar wasn't concerned with his own caste, but the Uttaboraa interested him greatly. If they were the masters of Atlantis, they were his enemy above all others. If he ever got the opportunity, he intended to kill them all.

10

T ar eagerly learned whatever Eregin had to teach.
The more he knew of Atlantis, its customs and
hierarchy, the better equipped he would be if he
survived to retirement.

Certain lessons grew in his mind. He often thought of
Eregin's explanation of gambling, and how betting made the
arena profitable. There was little money in admission fees,
but fortunes were routinely won and lost over a single bet.

The lesson about castes got Tar thinking of the future. To
get retribution from those whom he wished to destroy, he
would need power and influence. A common freeman,
Adigra-Kabra, had neither. He would have to rise from caste
to caste until such devils as Scimi and Heptumu were within
his reach. For the first time, Tar began to feel ambition. He
liked it.

The trouble was that he would not survive to retire. By
Heptumu's design, the combats became more dangerous by
the day. The heavy man said it was for the sake of spectacle,
as another large arena had recently opened in Atlantis. Audi-
ences were being drawn away and he was losing money. Tar

didn't believe it. The amphitheater was always full when he fought. If his master was losing money, the reason must be bad bets.

Tar led a recreation of the Red Tempest, a famous Atlantean sea battle from ancient times. The arena was filled with water pumped from the ocean below, and half-sized warships were floated upon it. These ships were ingeniously designed. They could be made to burst into flames, their masts to collapse, and finally to sink, without any true damage. They were all theatrical effects—only the deaths were real.

He swiftly learned that gathering a few good fighters, then leaping from vessel to vessel in the midst of all this chaos, killing as they went, worked perfectly well.

That experience made him want to learn how to sail a ship. There was no better prison than the open sea. It was pointless to consider—he didn't dream of tomorrow, he survived for today. The idea of sailing was as distant as the ass of the moon goddess.

In one particularly hellish fight, the arena floor was laced with hidden pits, in the bottoms of which were spear-points, poisonous snakes, and other hideous means of death. The pits were covered in thin reed mats, and the mats with sand, so even fighters as skilled as Tar himself were slain that day through sheer accident, falling through the floor of the arena.

When only a dozen slaves remained unhurt, they were removed from the pit. The wounded were left where they fell, begging for mercy or death, according to their injuries. Then Heptumu released the giant spiders. Their legs were as long as a man's arm, black and bristling. They ignored the dead and went straight for the wounded. They only hunted live prey.

The prey died with screams so terrible that Tar could not banish them from his ears—despite the fact that he had heard countless dying screams before. Big men died small deaths that day, veterans like himself who would soon have won their freedom. It angered him as it angered all the fighters. But they were slaves. Their anger meant nothing. They could not choose how or when to die. Only Heptumu did that.

When the guards herded the furious and bloody survivors of that day through the gate to the slave quarters, Tar was separated from the rest by well-armed men in an unfamiliar livery. Their helms were decorated with green-dyed plumes that extended down their backs, and their breastplates bore a crest of three golden angler-fish.

He looked to the overseer of the slaves, who had been writing down a list of casualties as the partially-eaten corpses were retrieved from the arena in baskets.

"What is this?" Tar said.

"Go with them, you fool," the overseer said, and winked bawdily. "It seems someone wants a private interview."

Tar did not know what this meant. Although his weapons had been taken away at the gate, he was prepared to fight bare-handed if need be. If he attacked these unknown men, Motia would surely pay the price as well as himself.

His natural curiosity demanded he see what this was about before he decided what to do. Although he was still seething with rage after the dishonorable fight, he kept outwardly calm and went where the men marched him, across the pit and directly away from the slave quarters.

TAR HAD NOT LEFT the premises of the fighting-pit since his arrival as a child. When the guards shoved him through a low side-gate into a walled yard that opened onto the public street, he nearly broke and ran for freedom.

He knew the street, having seen it from the roof of the

slave quarters. It was a broad and busy avenue that ran from the nearby harbor to the heart of Atlantis, where the palaces were clustered. Only for Motia's sake did he urge to escape. He clenched his teeth and his hands were fists. His muscles quivered with the effort of self-command.

He was taken to a rich palanquin placed on a stepped platform in the entrance of the yard. The carriage's long ivory traces were manned by a dozen slaves richly attired in green and gold. Its interior was hidden by shining cloth of Atlantis, a fabric formed from tiny polished rings. He could see nothing of what was inside.

"Get in," said the leader of his guards. "Behave like a newborn dolphin pup, or we will have your skin for boots."

Tar parted the shimmering curtains and stepped into the brightly-painted box. The inside was scented with spices, furnished with plump cushions and a chest of refreshments, and decorated with bouquets of exotic imported flowers. There was one occupant beside himself, a woman reclining on the cushions. She was clearly Uttaboraa.

11

"So this is the face of the Golden Prince," she said.

Tar remembered the manners he'd learned from Eregin. He must be on his best behavior, if only for Motia's sake. If he offended this woman, she could retaliate. Although there was only room to kneel inside the compartment, he bowed in the Atlantean way taught to him by the old man, with his left hand on his heart and his right arm hooked behind his back. He couldn't force himself to speak the formulaic greeting, however.

I live and die at your command would be a lie.

"A man of few words," the woman said into his silence. "I am Lady Rowana-Ya of House Mannon by House Chita. You will come with me to my palace for the afternoon. After today's butchery in the arena, I imagine you can do with some fresh air."

She rapped on the frame of the carriage with an intricately wrought fan. The palanquin swayed as the bearers settled the traces on their shoulders and began to move forward, through the entrance and into the street. All the while, the lady regarded Tar with careful attention, as if he were a a plate of unfamiliar but tempting meat. He returned her gaze.

She was in her middle years. Tar remembered a scrap of poetry old Eregin had read to him:

The afternoon of beauty
When the fields are ripe
And the orchards heavy with fruit.

It described her well.

She had the near-black lips, curling hair, and imperious nose of the native Atlantean. Her throat and arms were ringed with a fortune in metals and jewels, her naked breasts girdled up and powdered with gold. Her feet were rouged, which was the mark of marriage.

Despite the danger he sensed all around, desire plucked at Tar's groin.

He tore his eyes from her to take in their situation. The whole of the street was clearly visible through the cloth of Atlantis, as through a veil of gossamer. He knew that none could see inside, but felt exposed. The guardsmen marched on either side of the palanquin, crowds parting as they passed.

She leaned well forward so he could hear her breathy whisper over the din of the street.

"I am no danger to you."

"Do you attend the fights?" He blurted out.

She was getting much too close. She paused, inches from his face. He could smell clove oil on her tongue.

"Whenever you are on the sand," she said, coiling like a snake. "I have a private box in the first tier."

Sweat was prickling down his spine and drenching his ass.

"And you want to see me die up close, is that what this is about?"

"What do you mean?" She was genuinely surprised.

"I mean you can have me killed here by your men and feel my blood spray in your face."

She sighed deeply, then flumped herself back on the cushions. The bouquets of flowers nodded in sympathy. The seductress was gone, a disappointed court-matron in her place. Her eyes turned upon the passing street, but she was looking inwards.

"Twice a week I come to the arena to watch people die. Do you know why?"

She answered the question for him.

"Because I'm everything you think I am. The apotheosis of wealth, decadence, and privilege, spoiled beyond imagining and bored beyond endurance. A monster. You hate me, and you should."

Were it not for the spears beyond the curtains, he would give her a lesson in hate. She would never be bored again.

"I see the anger in those tawny eyes. You want to kill me. It would be so easy. You could crush my throat before I said a word to my guards, and probably get away."

The seductress had won again. She had desire on her side. Her thighs were restless against each other. She moistened her strong, dark lips with the point of her anointed tongue.

Now he understood what was happening. She was goading him. That's what got her off. No matter what temptation she threw in his way, he must not react.

Why had Heptumu put his most valuable fighter in this situation? Tar had to assume he was out of his mind.

"May I speak?" He said.

"Please, be my guest."

"Why did Heptumu allow this?"

"This visit? Money. Your master is in need of it."

"But he's rich," Tar said.

She laughed and rolled her eyes.

"There's a vulgar saying in Atlantis: 'A fish that eats gold is only rich until it shits.' I can't believe I just said that. How far the noble houses have fallen!"

She laughed as freely as if they were old friends. Perhaps that was because he could do nothing, yet she could do whatever she wanted. Slap him in the face, bite his nipples, piss on him, scratch—

He felt an anticipatory stirring inside his loincloth, and—with a bolt of panic—banished all such thoughts from his mind.

"What happens next?" he asked, his throat dry.

"Have you never done this before?" She laughed again, genuinely surprised. Her eyes were sparkling, the lines around them like echoes of her long black lashes. She leaned in close again, breasts spilling over her jeweled girdle.

"It is the custom of idle women—such as I—to entertain our heroes from time to time. Surely, many women have taken you home?"

"Never. They send gifts, but I have not met them."

She considered the implications of this, biting the edge of her thumb.

"That is very interesting," she said. "Why me, I wonder. It must be to do with my husband. He has an infinite quantity of money, but Heptumu has run out. I fit into this somehow."

Tar was tired of being toyed with. She might be a cat, but he was no mouse. The palanquin had stopped, caught in heavy traffic at a cross-street. Two goods-carts had gotten tangled up. Half the guards had gone ahead, shouting and shoving to clear the way. If he was to escape, there was no better moment.

She caught his arm with her hand, gripping tight.

"Please don't," she said. "You won't believe me, but I want you alive. I'm sorry I teased you."

He knew escape was futile. The only way to live through

the day was to play along. He settled against the cushions, resigned to his role.

"What is this entertainment you speak of? If you dan't want to see me die, what will it be? Do I kill one of your kitchen slaves for you?"

Rowana-Ya laughed deeply.

"No, nothing like that, no," she said. "I want you to fuck me out of my wits."

She rose to her knees, drawing so close their breaths mingled and he tasted clove. She ran her fingers over his dusty chest and arms like warm water.

"But not filthy like this," she added. "Your cock, at least, must be clean."

She slid her hand beneath his studded leather pteruges, under his loincloth, and drew out his rapidly swelling member.

"Gods be praised," she gasped.

She plunged her lips down the full length of his shaft until he was so hard it ached. Her teeth caught delicately at the rim of his cock. The muscles of his thighs and belly were rigid. He clenched his fists—she could do what she wanted, but he must not touch her.

He locked his entire body so that he would not move—and found he was looking into the face of a pretty young woman beyond the curtains. Her eyes were large and dark beneath thick brows. She was selling trinkets from a basket, and had stopped to wait for the traffic to clear. She gazed at the palanquin because it happened to be in front of her, and although she did not see him, she gazed straight at Tar.

He knew he was invisible to the woman outside. But as Lady Rowana-Ya gorged herself on his cock, it seemed to him the trinket-seller saw everything, and was indifferent—as if the sight of a rich woman with a pit fighter's blood-gorged member in her mouth was as commonplace as fish in the sea.

He felt a knot of delicious tension building up in his belly, and ground his teeth together.

Rowana-Ya was stroking him urgently with both hands now, her agile tongue scouring his rigid crown. The populace was only an arm's length away. Twitch open the curtain and see, people of Atlantis, how your high-caste women spend their afternoons!

Tar felt as if he had locked eyes with everyone in the crowd. His raging ecstasy was as public as death in the pit. His pleasure, like his pain, was there for the entertainment of all. The guards—who no doubt fantasized about this very thing with heir handsome mistress—the slaves, beggars, merchants, priests, and common folk: Enjoy the show.

Although it was Rowana-Ya who drove his cock to madness, it was the trinket-seller's gentle gaze that brought him to climax. His whole body stiffened. He gasped harshly, arched his back, and pumped jet after jet into his tormentor's eager throat, all the while staring into the young woman's eyes.

Rowana-Ya fell back on the cushions, panting for breath as the palanquin lurched back into motion. The trinket-seller was lost to view. Nobody had seen anything through the curtains, nor heard a sound with all the clamor of the street.

"I want you inside me now," Rowana-Ya whispered, licking her fingers clean. "I cannot bear it. But if I scream, my men will kill you, so we must wait."

12

———

Rowana-Ya occupied the remainder of the trip to the palace with light-hearted chatter, pointing out things of interest along the way. She served wine and fig-cakes to her guest. She behaved as if nothing out of the ordinary had happened. He began to wonder if he had dreamed of her eager mouth on his cock.

Tar distracted himself by looking at the strange costume of Atlanteans. His own people wore only a belt of woven reeds, men and women alike. The fashion among men of Atlantis was for a pair of sleeves tied behind the shoulders, stiff skirts to the knee, and a colorful sash at the waist to hold up their skirts.

Women wore longer skirts and decorated girdles that showed off their naked breasts—Rowana-Ya was a fine example. Poor women made do with a sash for the same purpose, and shawls over their shoulders. House slaves wore a string looped over one shoulder to denote their status as property. The poorer of both sexes wore only loincloths and shawls, and the poorest went naked.

Tar glimpsed the everyday Atlantis Eregin had described

during lessons. Although it was a huge place, every inch of it served a purpose. There were no vacant house-lots, no wilderness or fallow ground.

Common Atlanteans lived in bronze-walled *insulae*. These were apartment blocks raised haphazardly, floor-by-floor, until they leaned crookedly on each other over the narrow lanes like drunks. The poor lived beneath the shining streets, in basement tenements ten decks deep, with the poorest roosting among the seabirds at the margins, exposed to the wind and spray. The less people had, the closer to the ravenous sea they dwelled.

Of the richest quarters, Eregin had spoken little. So when Tar saw the palace in which Rowana-Ya spent her days, his mouth fell open with amazement. It stood among broad avenues with trees, fountains, and lawns that cooled and shaded the ways. There were tall, richly-sculpted walls of copper all around the palace, treetops visible in the gardens behind them. In the midst of the gardens, the palace itself rose up against the sky.

It was fantastical in shape, many-turreted, and clothed entirely in gold. From its highest tower rose one of the lofty masts, stayed by golden chains and arrayed with a collage of sails, each bearing the three angler-fish of the House Mannon. Many more palaces of similar magnificence stood on every side, each with its gardens, sky-piercing mast and blazoned sails.

Tar was dazzled by the wealth and grandeur of his surroundings. The masts were three times as high as the mightiest tree in his native forests. Every surface was richly carved and polished, and nothing was left to weather or decay. Tiny sailors worked among the rigging of the sails, so high in the air they looked like beetles.

Even as he drank in the spectacle of the palace, he was looking for possible routes of escape and places of concealment. He memorized any details of the terrain that might be of use. It was the Yunkai in him—his people cared nothing for wealth or spectacle. Survival was their primary concern.

The palanquin was borne into the palace grounds through a pair of gates in the outer wall, tall and broad enough for mastodons. The opening was fashioned to look as if the visitor was being swallowed by a fang-toothed, giant fish.

Sprawling gardens were laid on either hand, rich in flowers and tangles of exotic foliage. Although it was a work of artifice, the landscape was so cleverly wrought that it appeared to have been composed by nature.

The bearers carried the palanquin down a wide way surfaced with colorful shells and stones. A distant quarter of the garden was separate from the rest. Tar heard the sounds of strange animals from behind the wall.

"What beasts are there?" he asked.

"My husband's private menagerie. He collects plants and animals from every quarter of the world. You have probably fought some of his specimens in the arena. He sells the extras to your master."

Tar added her husband to the list of people he must kill.

"I have never set foot behind those walls, nor do I intend to," Rowana-Ya said. "But it can be seen from the windows of my private quarters. You'll have the view soon enough."

The palanquin came to rest in a courtyard fringed with tall green hedges. Tar emerged into a fragrant, green world of peace such as he did not knew could exist in Atlantis—or anywhere. He and Lady Rowana-Ya were escorted by the guardsmen to a stair of silver, which spiraled up to an entrance in the flank of the palace.

There were no openings in the ground level of the palace, Tar realized. Some thought had been given to fortification. It would be difficult to attack. But who would besiege a castle in the heart of an empire?

He tried to memorize the route they took, but there were so many rooms and levels he was soon lost. At last they came to a soaring, vaulted chamber. Its walls were inlaid with mother-of-pearl and framed by gaudy marble pilasters. The far end of the chamber was built around the foot of the mast.

A gilded cage suspended on chains stood against the mast. Tar followed Rowana-Ya into the cage. The guards remained behind, scowling up at him as the cage was hoisted high into the tallest tower by means of some concealed mechanism. It stopped precisely level with a floor near the top of the palace. The mast continued upward, piercing the roof.

There was no-one else on that floor, Tar sensed, unless his instincts failed him. He hadn't been truly alone since his arrival in Atlantis. Even in his private cell, there were guards outside, and the thin metal walls reverberated with sound. Here it was quiet and still. The absence of others was palpable.

"What manner of lawn is this?" he said, looking at the smooth purple sward beneath their feet. It covered the entire floor.

Rowana-Ya did not hide the amusement in her voice. "It is cloth woven from the hair of animals. A carpet. Come with me."

She took his hand—the first person to do so since he was very small—and guided him through a bell-shaped doorway into the semicircular chamber beyond. It was spacious and beautiful, the walls clad with inlays of pale blue silk. There were large, unglazed windows on all sides except the one through which they had come.

Tar crossed straight to the largest of the windows, extending from floor to ceiling. A balcony stood beyond. He stepped outside into the strong salt breeze and gaped at the view.

He could see half of Atlantis from there.

Directly below was the private menagerie, separate from the rest of the gardens. Its walls enclosed only a quarter of the palace grounds, yet there was ample space for woods, streams, and little stony hills, all standing among velvet-smooth lawns. There was even a lake with a pagoda in the center.

As impressive as it was, the palace was only one of many, each of equal grandeur, surmounted by blazoned sails and ringed around with pleasure gardens, with broad and orderly avenues between them.

The city wrapped around this golden district like an intricately embroidered tapestry. Every street was crammed with activity. First there were the dignified estates of merchants, money-lenders, and bureaucrats, each with its modest garden. Then came more crowded neighborhoods where the less-successful concealed their desperation and shared a garden square. Beyond these were heaped the tangled slums, where no-one concealed their desperation.

The slums were vast. They crawled all the way to the shores of Atlantis, which were scalloped with harbors. These were so full of ships and warehouses that the water in them could hardly be seen.

That was the end of the island, but its territory extended across the sail-feathered sea and over the fading horizon. Above it all was hung an afternoon sky of deepest blue, daubed with blushing clouds.

He felt Rowana-Ya's light hand on his shoulder.

"It is beautiful, is it not?" she said.

"I would give my eyes to see it drown."

"Then look away, Golden Prince."

He turned his back to the view. She was standing close behind him. She unclasped her girdle. Her skirts fell around her feet. She was naked.

13

He took her by the throat and pressed his mouth to hers. She broke away and fell to her knees, dragging his pteruges and loincloth down. His rigid cock swayed free and stood straight up against his belly. He felt her breath upon it, but she did not touch. He took her by the hair and dragged her to her feet, then crushed her in his arms.

There was a richly-clothed bed across the room, but his desire was too urgent. He grasped her full thighs and lifted her onto a table laden with cosmetics. Jars of oil, color, and perfume spilled to the floor, soaking the carpet.

For an instant Tar saw through the red fog of lust—he was on the precipice between madness and death, bruising the tender flesh of a woman whose slightest whim could mean his destruction. He should back away. He should grovel in the litter of pots and jars at her feet and beg for his life.

He did not. He pushed her trembling legs apart until she whimpered. Her cunt opened to him. He locked his eyes with hers and waited, his cock jumping with every beat of his heart.

"Please," she whimpered. "Please."

He filled her completely. She cried out as if beaten, but hooked her heels around his hips and forced him deeper.

The pain of the arena was forgotten. Tar's rage and fear were transformed into the delicious agony of passion. In *this* arena, he needed no weapon but a heavy cock. He fucked her on the table until it collapsed, then fucked her on the floor in a pool of scented oil. Their slippery bodies gleamed.

He flipped her over so that she was groveling with her face in the carpet. He fucked her savagely until her haunches bounced against her back. Every stroke was a killing blow. She should have died. Instead, she came, and came again, until she wept and begged for mercy. He drew himself out of her, and laughed.

"There's no mercy in all of Atlantis."

She raised her ass in the air and opened her buttocks to him.

"Then slay me."

He slathered his iron-hard member with oil. If this woman wanted punishment, she had chosen her persecutor well. He had only just begun.

THEY LAY PANTING on the carpet. The chamber was in ruins. What wasn't broken had been knocked over, there were drifts of feathers from disemboweled cushions strewn across the ruined carpet, and impressions of her breasts and buttocks were printed on the silken walls. The only part of the room that had escaped his wrath was the bed itself.

He saw that tears were trickling over the fine lines around her eyes.

"Why do you weep?"

"Because I feel joy."

"Weeping is for sorrow."

She propped herself up on an elbow and looked at him with something like tenderness.

"How often have you experienced joy?"

"Never."

"That is why I weep. It's rare."

He didn't know what she was talking about. It didn't matter. He was fairly certain he'd met her expectations, and that she wouldn't have him killed. That was good enough for him. She watched his face as he considered his situation, then interrupted his thoughts:

"Would you like to bathe with me?"

14

———

Her bathing-room was next to the bedchamber. It was entirely of white marble veined with sparkling agate. The bath was fashioned in the shape of a gigantic seashell, deep and broad. Tar lay on one end with his hands folded behind his head. He had never enjoyed hot water before. His muscles relaxed so deeply it felt as if his very bones were softening.

Rowana-Ya lounged on the opposite end, immersed to her chin, her blushing face made hazy by scented steam. She stroked his feet with her own. She was happy to do the talking, for she seldom met anyone who listened so intently.

"There are no men like you in in my caste. The high-born insinuate themselves into bed with hints and flattery, then make love like pick-pockets stealing a purse. You fuck like you fight, without remorse. I thought you meant to murder me with pleasure, Golden Prince."

Tar said nothing, because she was right.

"My husband, Count Jaff He-Ah, built this room to make his cock stand up for me. That bed is equipped with every tool of pleasure. It was all for nothing. I've never seen him fully hard. Only cruelty stirs his loins, but as I am niece to King Harpan, he doesn't dare to injure me. Instead he schemes with my enemies to ensure I am unhappy."

"He will kill me when he learns of this meeting," Tar said.

She laughed scornfully, but the scorn was not for him.

"You do not know the ways of Atlantis. Have you heard *The Queen's Lament*? It is a very old song."

Tar shook his head. The only Atlantean songs he knew were filthy chanties croaked out in the fighter's quarters. She began to sing, her voice as clear and sorrowful as a caged bird:

"My realm extends from sea to shore
With riches I am full replete;
The golden crown, Atlantis, lies
Below my new-blushed feet.

THEN WHY, *fair queen, do you so weep?*
An empire great you wed
We shiv'ring wretches naked are
And make the streets our bed.

CONSORT *to the king am I,*
Sea and sky at my command
But love to him I cannot give
Nor in return demand.

FAIR LADY, *if a kingdom great*
Is not what you desire,
Then why a cold heart married you
When love you most require?

· · ·

I JOINED my house to his, because
  Of blood is empire built
  Great blood in noble veins combined,
  Low blood in battle spilt.

MY TRUE LOVE was a soldier brave
  And died in my husband's war;
  To join my love, I'll pierce my heart
  Whence crimson rubies pour."

TAR CONSIDERED the meaning of her song. "You marry only for property and power, not love?"

"The Uttaboraa, grand old families like mine, must do. It's how we keep the property and power to ourselves. The middling classes marry for love, and the poor don't marry at all."

"Then your husband will *surely* kill me," Tar said.

If he was to die, he intended to do so in combat, not balls-out in a perfumed bath. He stood up dripping, wondering where he'd flung his fighting-harness.

"Don't be a fool," Rowana-Ya laughed. "He can have you destroyed no matter where you are—in Atlantis, on the sea, or on dry land."

"Then why you have cursed me to be slain?"

"Your ignorance is boundless! This is no wrongdoing; monogamy is unknown here. My husband cares not whom I fuck. He has a harem of his own."

"But I am a slave."

She rose from the bath and dried them both with soft animal furs.

"We may share our flesh with anyone we wish, be it a

prince or pit-fighter, a pithecus or a porpoise. The only thing we cannot share is our hearts."

He understood now. "That is the meaning of the song," he said. "Love is worth more than a kingdom."

"Do you agree?" she asked.

"It's nonsense. I'd give up love for a crust of bread."

"Then you have not tasted love," she said. "The song is a true story. Opa of Atlantis was our fifth queen, many centuries ago. She loved a common soldier, and the tyrant king was jealous. So he sent three thousand men into a battle they could not win, her lover among them. When Queen Opa heard of the massacre, she took her own life. But this conversation has turned gloomy. I am chilled. Warm my bed before you leave, Golden Prince. It's the only piece of furniture left."

15

———————

That evening, Tar lay on the floor of his cell and considered the events of the day. Even the memory of the pretty trinket-seller's eyes could not stir his well-punished prick. He liked the lady Rowana-Ya despite himself.

Although she was more than twice his age, she was a tireless lover, mature enough to know what she liked from a man, and confident enough to demand it. When she wasn't draining his balls, she was interesting to listen to, observant and cynical. She reminded him of old Eregin in that way—and only in that way.

Most of the slave-whores with which pit-fighters were furnished were young, terrified and sickly, kidnapped by men like Scimi. Tar wouldn't lie with them. He remembered the terror and pain of the sea voyage to Atlantis. There could be no pleasure in rape for him, no matter how lowly the woman. Yet he had violated Rowana-Ya in ways the pirates had violated him.

Why had he not hesitated to sodomize her? He had slapped her, bruised her, knotted his fists in her hair and throat-fucked her until the paint on her eyelashes ran down her cheeks. Why was he not troubled by this? He decided it was because she had demanded the punishment herself. Men had begged him to end their suffering in the arena, and he had done so. Perhaps there *was* mercy in him, after all.

He could not fully understand why she had sung that ancient ballad. It seemed like a strange confession. Did she love a soldier in her husband's garrison? He would never know. Anyway, his balls were as empty as a beggar's purse, and he was grateful for that.

As he was reflecting on the events of the day, Motia entered the cell, escorted in by the smirking guards. Word had spread that Tar had visited the lady of House Mannon, whose insatiable lust was famed in all of Atlantis. He saw from Motia's hard expression that she had heard the news as well. She greeted him as always, and tidied the cell, then shed her tunic for sleep. But instead of the bed, she lay down on the floor beside him.

"What is this?" Tar asked.

Tar thought his cock would never rise again, but he was wrong. She teased it back to life, and was soon riding him to ecstasy. After that night, she was no longer shy.

Heptumu visited the cell the following day. Fighters rested on the day after a combat. It was lucky for Tar that this was so, because he was so spent from lovemaking that old Eregin could have beaten him hand-to-hand.

The heavy man had again brought wine, which Tar drank thirstily.

"I am informed you pleased the lady of house Mannon yesterday," Heptumu said, and raised his cup by way of salute. His peculiar odor filled the room.

"I pleased her as many times as all the fingers on my hands and both thumbs of another."

He hadn't meant it to be funny, but Heptumu roared with laughter until his eye-paint also ran with tears.

"Marvelous," he wheezed. "I'm told she's been forced to replace that priceless carpet of hers. In fact she has offered to buy you from me, and has made a very generous offer. I'd consider it, except now she'll pay twice as much for a single afternoon."

"If I die tomorrow, there's not another half-copper in it for you. The fights have become games of chance, not skill."

Heptumu looked at him slyly. He was twisting the heavy rings on his fingers—a nervous habit.

"Do you know what insurance is?"

"I've never heard of it," Tar said, and held out his cup for more wine.

"It's a form of gambling. I agree to pay a man a modest sum for every week you survive. He agrees to pay me an enormous sum if you die. Whether you live or die, I'll be richer tomorrow."

Tar considered this, and decided he would add the insurance man to his list of people to kill. Heptumu, perhaps sensing Tar's dangerous mood, changed the subject.

"I'm told you're not the only one of my slaves who doesn't like the new combats I've devised," said Heptumu.

"You might as well choose who lives and dies with a throw of the dice."

Heptumu refilled their cups.

"Here's the trouble, Golden Prince. I've got expensive plans. To finance my plans, I need to ensure that the betting is heavy. If the same fighters win every time, nobody will wager on the rest. So I introduce variables to make the outcome of fights impossible to guess. Any businessman would do the same."

Tar struggled to express what was wrong with this, but he didn't have the words. The Yunkai had no concept of fairness, or he'd have said it was unfair. They did, however, understand honor.

"It's dishonorable."

"Slaves have no claim on honor," Heptumu said.

He drained his cup and left the cell. His stink lingered long afterwards.

16

Tar was convinced Heptumu had gone mad. In the following weeks, the fights became carnage. On one occasion, the pit was swarming with thousands of starving rats, the fighters armed only with hammers. The one who killed the most rats was the winner. The ones who were eaten alive were the losers.

Then the big man invented a way for the audience to participate, shooting lightweight arrows from the stands at a bronze coin per shaft. This proved immensely popular with the public, at great cost to the fighters in the pit.

All of the fighters grumbled about escaping, but there was no escaping the island Atlantis. Even if they rose up against their oppressor and broke free, there was nowhere to go.

With three months left to retirement, Tar felt the chill of the underworld upon his neck. His death was close. Its shadow dimmed the sun. The arena itself became a twilight. He was convinced that Heptumu needed him to die a slave—probably for the insurance money he'd mentioned.

Motia would be made a sex slave again, or be sent down to the pontoons. There she would suffer in the icy-cold gloom under Atlantis, mopping grease on gigantic fittings until she drowned or was crushed, like the woman Tar had seen die the day he arrived.

He would not live to retire. It was time to escape.

For this reason, he began training Motia in self-defense. He did it always in secret, in his cell—if she showed promise as a fighter, she would be sent into the arena herself.

Mixed-sex fights among breeding aged slaves was illegal, but there were many all-women fights. The female fighters were kept in separate quarters and did not mingle with the males. Tar was glad of this. He'd witnessed the women commit acts of incredible savagery. There were fights in which their hands were tied and they bit each other to death.

Because Atlantis was a structure, not a natural environment, he taught Motia how to use walls, doorways, and corners to aid her in defense. He trained her to duck out and stab, then duck back, to lie in wait, to use a confined space to advantage. As his cell was small, he could do nothing else in any case.

She was strong enough, but lacked the taste for killing. She didn't want to hurt him when they sparred, and stopped fighting when he let her strike him. That would get her killed. A thousand things would get her killed. For a month they trained in secret. She got stronger and better and more ruthless, but she was no killer. There wasn't time for more.

It was nearing summer. The seas were as calm as they ever would be, with countless ships coming and going, like ants tending to an enormous golden queen. Good weather and long evenings had relaxed the people of Atlantis, insofar as they ever relaxed. Heptumu's guards felt it, too, with the balmy breezes carrying away the stink and noise from the streets around. They were less alert.

With seven weeks left in his career as a pit-fighter, Heptumu pitted Tar against six men. They were armed and he was not. He quickly armed himself by killing one of the men, but then Heptumu sent in a replacement. Tar slew several hands of men that day. It was perfectly obvious that he was supposed to die. After that combat, he resolved they would escape by the roof on the following night, when the moon would be gone from the sky.

He had no fear of his guards. He knew them well by now, and knew their weaknesses. They would die, and their armor would make fine disguises. Then, after a quick march to the nearest harbor, they would stow away aboard the ship soonest departing, and Atlantis would become a cruel memory.

"Will we die tomorrow?" Motia asked.

They were lying in the straw, having enjoyed the more tender style of lovemaking she had taught him, as he had taught her fighting.

"If not tomorrow, the next day, or another," Tar said.

"I am afraid to die."

"That is because you are no longer afraid to live," he said.

A SUMMER TEMPEST BLEW IN, which perfectly suited Tar's plans. The storm made the night dark, and extinguished the oil lamps that lit the streets.

There was no natural source of fresh water in Atlantis. Every exterior surface was designed to collect rainwater, channeling it into large open-topped cauldrons at street level, from which it could be drawn for use. Wealthy houses imported their water from the mainland, by way of ships equipped with enormous river-filled tanks. The common folk made do with seawater that had been turned to steam and precipitated into another vessel. It was always sour. They bathed and washed their clothes in seawater.

So when it rained, night or day, everyone would rush

outside to wash themselves and their possessions in the sweet, clean water. That included slaves who had access to the outdoors, of which Tar was one. Followed by his two guards, he ascended to the roof and bade Motia wash their garments in a tub of rainwater. The guards, who thought of Tar almost as a friend, took the opportunity to wash their own linens—which required setting aside their weapons.

Tar was naked, washing himself with harsh fatty soap, when he saw that both guards had their backs to him. They were scrubbing their breeches alongside Motia at the tub. Silently he took up one of the short swords at their heels, and killed them both with swift stabs to the neck. The look of surprise on their dead faces was gratifying. Tar didn't consider them friends at all.

He showed Motia how to dress in armor, then clad himself. She was far too small for hers, but it wasn't important.

"Now we jump," he said.

"We'll break our bones!" she objected.

"Not if we jump into those barrels of rainwater," he said, and pushed her over the parapet of the roof. He followed her a moment later.

She was furious, sputtering and coughing. He helped her climb out of the cauldron. As soon as their feet touched the street, she forgot the fall and focused her attention on their escape. She knew the streets around the fighting pits better than Tar, as domestic slaves such as she were permitted to leave their quarters.

By now the storm was roaring, with high winds and sheets of rain that slapped their faces like an open hand.

She guided him through narrow, half-flooded alleys that sometimes became slippery stairs, and other times suspension bridges across gaps in Atlantis's decks. Only strokes of lightning lit their way. They came at last to a doorway that led under the streets. Until then, they had run into no patrols and saw few citizens—nearly everyone had gone to their roofs, or was gathered in the open squares where the rain fell most plentifully. Tar was glad to get under the streets and out of the blinding rain.

A piercing horn-note bellowed out over the storm, distant but loud. It came from the quarter they had fled. The alarm was raised.

17

———

"We will have to fight," Tar said, and drew his stolen sword.

"We're halfway to the harbor," Motia said. "They won't find us."

He took her by the shoulders and drew her face close, so that she could see him despite the dark.

"Motia, listen to me. Assume anyone we meet is the enemy. I go first. You keep watch behind."

There had only been one attempt to escape in Tar's time in the pits, made by a criminal sentenced to fight—a native who knew Atlantis well. That same horn had sounded, and the fugitive's head stood on a spike in front of the fighter's quarters before the day was done.

The odds of success were not good, Tar knew, but it was better to choose his own manner of death. If he had doomed Motia to the same fate, at least she might be spared further suffering. It was too late to doubt.

They followed a vague course through a confusion of handmade streets and hovels below Atlantis's surface. The wind shrieked and buffeted. The furious waves sucked and boomed against the pontoons beneath their feet like gigantic monsters that could smell their blood. Most of the residents of these foul places had gone above to make use of the rain, but they passed many doorways behind which were ragged huddles of people trying to stay warm, if not dry, which was impossible in those depths of the city. The lung-clotting reek of them was so strong it overcame the stink of mildew and rotten fish.

The fugitives came to a narrow alley of taverns, and to the reek was added the smell of *muyu*, or fermented seaweed— the strong, foul drink of choice for the poor. Tar could not swallow the stuff. The taverns were noisy with trade, but no-one was in the street. What light there was came from grease lamps.

Over the storm came the sound of singing, drunken voices shouting one of the call-and-response songs beloved of Atlanteans:

"*I* CAN HARDLY WALK

    Since she took my cock

    And used it to pump water," The solo voice sang.

    The chorus replied:

    "*Is that why you shuffle, oh*

    Like a wounded buffalo,

    Since you met the captain's daughter?

    The soloist came in again:

    "*Nay! My cock's as large*

    As a barracks barge

    It's a wonder I can totter!"

A ROAR OF LAUGHTER FOLLOWED.

"Now," Tar said, and they hurried down the alley.

Red light spilled out of the doorway opposite the noisy tavern, and two king's men emerged, armored and armed. They held an emaciated boy by the arms. They were between Tar and the harbor.

"You'll learn not to steal one finger at a time," said the larger of the two soldiers to the boy, and cuffed him across the mouth.

They saw Tar and Motia, only feet away. They thought nothing of *him*. He was a guard of the arena, as far as they knew. But women didn't do such work.

"Who the hell is she," said the first soldier.

"My woman," Tar said.

"Why is she dressed up like that?" the second guard wanted to know.

"Because we just escaped the fighting-pit," Tar said, and drew sword.

The soldiers were seasoned fighters themselves, but the alley was narrow and they had come to arrest a child, not to fight a butcher. The fight was over before the small thief was out of sight around the corner. In moments, the bigger man was missing his jaw, and the other was blinking at the stump of his arm. Tar cut the jawless man's throat and looked to Motia.

"Blood your knife," he said.

She gathered her will, breathing hard, then plunged her dagger into the one-armed guard's neck. For a moment she looked horrified. Blood sprayed out, the man writhed. Then she stabbed him again and again until he was still. The rain mingled with the blood on her face. She looked at Tar, and he saw something new in her eyes: Triumph.

"I hear the open ocean," she said. "We must hurry."

She ran close behind him. They came to the end of the crudely-built dwelling blocks under the streets, continuing into the uninhabited region of guano-streaked bronze buttresses that fringed the island. The footing was treacherous. They went swiftly, slipping and skidding.

They threaded their way along catwalks and platforms installed so that slaves could maintain the web of giant struts and girders that braced the streets above. Soon they caught glimpses of the harbor, with long ships bucking and plunging like toy boats against their moorings. The light came from windproof lamps used to keep thieves out of the warehouses. Phosphorescence flashed blue and green to mark the churning waterline, and lightning turned the night to day at irregular intervals.

He dared to think they would survive long enough to hide themselves in one of those ships. The docks were completely empty—waves crashed over them. Only a madman or a fugitive would dare go down there. If they were lucky enough to choose a ship that didn't come loose and dash itself to pieces against the pontoons before the storm was over, they might yet put Atlantis behind them.

Dizzy ramps and ladders led down toward the waterfront. There, warehouses were bolted to the faces of the pontoons, the docks moored in front of them on barrel-floats that mimicked the motion of the waves. There were lights inside the warehouses, but Tar doubted anyone could see a thing outside.

They descended a spiral stair that wound around a column overlooking the harbor. It ended in a platform railed with rope, low enough that the biggest waves threw spume into their faces. From there, a ladder of chains would take them to the docks. He turned to Motia.

"We are close," he said. "We'll board the nearest ship, the one with the bird's head on the prow. It isn't kicking as much as the others."

Motia put her icy hand on his cheek.

"I am so cold, Tar Yunkai of Men. Hold me."

Her teeth were chattering and she shivered as if with marsh-fever. He pulled her to him and she threw her arms around his waist, the sleeves of her outsized guard's uniform flopping past the tips of her fingers.

"Tell me we will live," she said.

Tar did not know if they would. He could not lie to her.

"We are free," he replied. "It's better to be free for one minute than slave for a lifetime."

"I know it is true, but I'm not as brave as you," she said. "I am afraid."

"I'm afraid too."

"That cannot be."

"Every time I step into the pit, I am afraid. But my gods despise cowards. So I overcome my fear and fight. If we die bravely, we die well."

Lightning flashed. He saw her face, filled with hope. He'd said the right words. He was glad.

"I must speak my heart," she said. "Golden Prince, I—"

Her eyes flew wide. She opened her mouth and tried to breathe, but could not. She stumbled out of his arms.

"Motia!" Tar shouted, reaching for her.

She could not hear him. She tumbled off the platform into the raging sea, an arrow buried in her back.

The arrow had been loosed when the lightning flashed. He saw there were soldiers gathered high up on the rim of the upper deck. He could hear them shouting.

They would have known where the fugitives were going, and only had to lie in wait. No need for pursuit. Another arrow caught the meat of his shoulder. He tore it out, his sight red with rage, and ducked behind the column. More arrows clattered against the metal.

There was no course of action but to fight the soldiers as they came down. He was trapped and he would die in this miserable place, as Motia had. But he could rob his enemies of the satisfaction of killing him.

He stripped out of his sodden armor, commended Motia's soul to his indifferent gods, and hurled himself after her into the void.

18

———

Tar did not die that night. He still knew little of Atlantis. He did not know that the entire island was skirted with countless nets, weighted down to catch the schooling fish that swarmed beneath it.

When he hit the water, the icy blow cleared his mind but left his body half-paralyzed, as if he'd been slapped by a giant's hand. He struggled numbly in the churn and was plunged and thrown about until his strength was gone. The surge dragged him far below the surface and he felt death embrace him. Even as he consigned his soul to oblivion, he was flung upward again, and tumbled into the nets.

They tangled around his limbs, the fine wire of which they were woven cutting him in a hundred places. He was trapped there, and only his nose and mouth could reach the surface in the troughs between waves.

He had killed Motia, as surely as with a sword thrust. He had killed himself. He would die unfree like the slave he was —a captive not of men, but a fishing net. He wanted to suck the ocean into his lungs and hasten his destruction. He could not. His burning will demanded he live. His *gods* demanded he live.

He gulped air when he could, and drowned between times, and finally lost consciousness in a chaos of pain and sorrow and rage.

THEY DID NOT PUT slaves on trial in Atlantis. To be accused was to be guilty. A fighter of Tar's status would ordinarily be executed in the pit by his own master's hand—the crowds loved to see it. But he had been captured by the crown's soldiers, not Heptumu's, so his fate was to be determined by the king's decree. It was the same Atlantean law that had spared him from Scimi's justice years ago.

King Harpan of Atlantis didn't execute slaves. A steady supply of expendable bodies was needed for the dangerous work of maintaining the pontoons and rigging.

Tar was hauled up out of the waves, imprisoned in a cell too small to lie down in, and left there until he healed enough stand on his own.

In that dark, damp compartment, he learned that hell was made of thoughts. His people didn't believe in an afterlife. Life began from nothing and ended the same way. Atlanteans, because they were fools, thought there was more to come.

Their religion was too complicated for Tar—or rather, he wasn't interested enough to grasp the details. Old Eregin had told him of it, mostly so that he didn't offend people with his ignorance.

Most of their gods were sea-gods, foremost among them Mazo-Mari. When Atlanteans died, their souls stepped into a celestial ship named Atlax. The ship voyaged across the oceans of the dead. Those who were worthy in life had plenty of galley slaves at the oars and wind in the sails, and soon came to paradise, which according to Eregin was a great deal like Atlantis, except it smelled better and there were no poor people.

Those who were not virtuous sailed around in circles for a thousand years before reaching paradise. Their ship leaked and the sails held no wind. The ships of those who did evil—which coincided exactly with breaking the laws of Atlantis—would sink, and their souls would be devoured by sharks for a million years.

Tar had no concept of thousands or millions, except that they were as numerous as leaves in the forest. But he came to understand that time could pass so slowly that an hour would last as long as Eregin's life.

It was Motia who tormented him like the sharks in the sea of the dead. Every moment he was awake, he saw her eyes widen in the instant of death. He saw her plunge into the chaos of the sea. He cursed himself until the words had no meaning any longer. He beat the walls of his cell with his fists and battered his skull against them until he could not feel the pain. No matter what he did, Motia died again, and again, and again.

It was no more than two weeks before he was taken from that place, yet he had circled the sea of the damned for an eternity. His captors bound him with chains. He did not object. They marched him beneath the streets to a stockade full of other wretches like himself, condemned to the worst existence Atlantis could provide. Most were men, but there were women as well. None were children. Atlantis had other uses for them.

A long rawhide shirt of sealskin was issued to every slave at the direction of the overseer there. He was a powerful, flat-headed man in sharkskin breeches.

"You're Dugra now, less than the animals that wore those skins," he shouted to his shivering, filthy charges. "I'll give you the bad news first. You'll never see the sun again. Your home is inside the pontoon you're assigned to, the coldest and stinkingest hell there is. You'll work until your strength is gone. You'll eat what the rats can't swallow."

A ripple of dismay whispered through the prisoners. The overseer was pleased.

"Here's the good news. You'll all be dead before your sister's cunt bleeds twice, so you won't suffer for long. Form rows along those lines on the floor, and do it quick, because from now on, the lash does the talking, not me."

To underline the point, a slave-master with a rusty beard as long as his arm stepped out in front of the convicts. He lashed the man nearest to him with a whip of knotted gut. It cut a strip out of the flesh of his target, showing white until the blood came. The man fell to his knees, screaming.

"And if you don't like the lash," Red-Beard said, "Complain to the fishes."

He caught the whipped man by his hair and hauled him to a hatch in the floor, then kicked him in the face. The slave fell through the hatch. A short, echoing scream, a splash, and the demonstration was over.

The convicts shuffled into rows. They were chained together about the neck, ten per gang. Each gang was assigned to a pontoon, then beaten into motion by the slave-masters. The gangs spread out under the city. Their assigned pontoons were scattered beneath every part of the island. Some marched for two days.

Tar was at the rear of his gang, the last one in the row. He trudged in time to the others. It was his bad luck that Red-Beard was their escort.

By the time they were near their destination, all of the convicts in the gang had suffered at least one lash. Tar received several. Red-Beard knew whom he was, and men with small power love to punish those who frighten them.

Tar's reputation as the Golden Prince was sufficient to attract the whip no matter how well he behaved. He worried that his list of men to kill would grow longer than he could remember.

The chain gang halted on top of the assigned pontoon, which was encrusted with bird guano, slimy and icy-cold. This far from the open sea, the floats were not decorated, as none but the slaves would ever see them. Chains with links as big as fishing-boats joined them together. Everything was built on such a vast scale that human beings looked like sand fleas.

Tar wondered where he was in terms of the city above. He imagined the palace of House Mannon somewhere nearby, Lady Rowana-Ya entertaining some new warrior in her bed while he rotted far below.

Two soldiers emerged from a crudely-made cabin of scrap metal that stood in the middle of the broad, flat top of the pontoon. Tar had never seen a more disreputable pair. They must be down there as punishment, he thought. Deserters or cowards. That might be of use to him. He had no intention of dying beneath Atlantis.

If he had not died after his leap into the sea—as certain a death as could be imagined—then the gods expected him to live, whether he wanted to or not. Whatever their reasons, he must endure.

The Yunkai's gods were uncaring of their children, but sometimes had use for them.

Red-Beard aimed one final lash at Tar.

"That one—show him no kindness," the man muttered to the guards, and spat in his beard.

Red-Beard turned back the way they'd come, ready to

hone his whip-skills on the next batch of less-than-human Dugra.

The guards didn't even glance at Tar. Their sprits were broken. If he had the chance, they'd die easily enough. The challenge would be in keeping his own spirit alive.

So Tar began the cruelest existence known to Atlantis, a fate that did more to keep the population docile than any other punishment. It was better to live in the lowest servitude, even to die in the fighting-pits, than to perish in the dripping darkness between Atlantis and the sea. The first day, one of his fellow slaves died. His legs were torn in half when a section of the pontoon's skin gave way. The soldiers unlocked his neck-chain and the corpse fell into the water, to be devoured in moments by dark, twisting shapes below the surface.

A shaven-headed woman was added to the chain in his place, and the gang spent the next several days hammering the sheets of metal back together. The guard shack contained tools, grease, and sacks of huge rivets. None of the gang knew how to do the work, so the results wouldn't last long.

The days were spent in exhausting labor, dangling over the bottomless, black sea. There would be no surviving a fall into that water. The currents were fierce, and whirlpools as deep as caves would form when the waves were at their highest. Sometimes huge fins and tentacles would break the surface below. Old and injured predators, unable to hunt as before, had learned they could still find a morsel beneath the island.

Occasionally, fine boats would pass among the pontoons. They were gaily decorated and bore the crests of noble families. The boats followed fixed courses, drawn along on cables that ran through pulleys set in the lowest parts of the pontoons. The boats were fully enclosed, so Tar never saw who was aboard—but he knew it would be the decadent Uttaboraa.

Tar's gang slept inside the assigned pontoon, an echoing, cathedral-sized space with buttresses running in all directions to brace up the outer skin. Their home was a beam just wide enough to sleep on, a few feet above the foul, greasy bilge that sloshed around the bottom. If anyone rolled off, it pulled the rest down as well, and they would choke in the slime until they were able to crawl back up again.

In the morning, if morning it was, they would wake to the scream of hinges, and a hatch in the top of the pontoon would clang open. It was so high above them it looked no bigger than a gold coin. One of the guards would thrust a torch into the opening and drop a ladder made of chains. Hindered by their own chains, the gang would climb the ladder. The slaves were issued their tools, usually mops and grease, and went where they were told, to work until their strength was gone.

At night the guards placed a tub of fish entrails and seaweed by the hatch. The slaves ate it or starved. Tar forced himself to eat as much as possible, because he would need strength. Seaweed was a common part of the pit fighter's diet, and was nutritious. So he ate more of that. It was also less disgusting than shark's bowels. To drink, they got brackish water distilled from the sea, which they supplemented by licking the condensation from the interior of the pontoon.

Once their eating-time was over, a matter of five minutes, the slaves descended the chain ladder again, groping around in the darkness until they reached the beam and lay down to shiver and mourn. Tar marked the days for a while, but lost track. The only way to know how much time had passed was to see how many of his original gang were still alive. Four remained, including himself.

His mind was not working as well as it had by then. He attempted to come up with plans of escape, but the chain around his waist would not break, and the locks that secured him were equally strong. The guards did not have the keys to them, so they were of little use. Only overseers had keys, like Red-Beard, whom Tar had not seen again since his arrival.

He had never cared for mere hope—the dream of idle folk —but he had tasted ambition, which is hope with a sword in its hand. In that cold, wet hell, his ambitions seemed futile. They faded until he had nothing left but hatred. He wanted to see the entire island set to the torch and sunk beneath the waves. Then he wouldn't need to hunt down those whom he wished to kill. He'd kill everyone who dwelled there, and their sea-gods could decide which of their supplicants died worthily, and which must be devoured by sharks for a million years.

The monotony, the lack of day and night—here was the sea of the dead. The hell Atlanteans spoke of was beneath their feet. He suffered and toiled and became the animal his masters called him. Thoughts no longer came to him. His curiosity had withered away. His furious will, like his skin, was corroded into mush by salt, damp, and pain.

Then he saw something that awakened his mind. One day his gang was sent to a new place overlooking a monstrous shaft of some blackened metal. It descended into the restless sea, as big around as a fortified tower. It would sometimes rotate a few degrees with a sound like an earthquake. While they mopped grease, he asked the bald woman in front of him what it was.

"A rudder," she said. "To steer Atlantis. Every palace has one under its mast. They go down as far as the masts go up."

"Atlantis can be *steered?*"

Tar had never thought of this. He assumed the island drifted wherever the wind blew the sails. The woman tried to laugh, but only made a dry croaking sound.

"The world doesn't fear this empire because it floats around aimlessly like a jellyfish. They fear it because it can show up off any coast, and lay waste to we who live there. Thus was I taken for a slave, and stabbed my master."

"Rule the sea and you rule the world." Tar felt his mind working for the first time since that dark eternity began.

The woman spat into the darkness below.

"That's right. They claim this place is a city, an island, and a nation. But Atlantis is a *warship.*"

That same day, Tar almost died. Three of the others on the chain did, including the woman to whom he had spoken. One of the giant chains broke free somewhere high above them in the darkness with a sound like a mountain splitting open. The chain came roaring down, crushing the flank of the pontoon, and smeared the front of the gang to paste. The woman's head remained in her collar, but the rest of her was gone.

Had the neck-chains not been shattered along with the bodies, they all would have perished. Tar used all of his strength to pull the survivors behind him to safety on a dangling scrap of the catwalk they'd been standing on. He didn't do it to save them—he did it to keep their weight from breaking his neck.

He threw the bald woman's head overboard, after the rest

of her. To his fury, the chain was still secure around his throat. Otherwise he could have taken the chance to break free, slay the guards, and disappear up into the belly of Atlantis. Instead, the survivors crawled back to the top deck and sprawled panting and blood-spattered on the guano-encrusted bronze, the guards staring at them as if they were ghosts.

Tar knew his gods wanted him to live, but that chain had carried a message with it. He must act soon to do their will, whatever it was. He couldn't satisfy them if he remained where he was. He resolved to kill the guards the following morning and use what tools they had to break the lock. If that didn't work, he'd kill the other slaves as well, cut their bodies apart, and carry the chain with him.

As they were too few to work, the slaves were sent back down into the echoing pontoon. It was flooding. The skin was too torn for such feeble repairs as they could manage. Dim light filtered in through the rents in the bronze. They slept much closer to the hatch this time, as their old roost was underwater. Tar forced himself to sleep as much as he could while they waited. He would need the strength.

There was no measure of time where they were, but it seemed too soon when the hatch creaked open again. The torchlight flared red, then something blotted out the opening for a moment. A shape fell through and splashed into the filth below, which was much closer than it had been only hours before. The pontoon was sinking.

Moments later, a crude bottle-lamp was lowered on a cord. It dangled above the upturned faces of the chain gang. Tar saw in the feeble light that one of the guards was floating in the bilge, his throat cut.

"Which of you is the Golden Prince?" Came a voice from the hatch.

Tar didn't speak, but another of the slaves pointed him

out with a trembling finger. An arrow hissed down and killed that slave. The rest died in the same way, leaving only Tar. He Fought to remain standing despite the corpses dangling around his neck, and glared up at the hatch, raging to die such a useless death.

There came another hiss, and a dart struck him in the skull. He wrenched it free—it was light, hardly longer than his finger—but felt his scalp burning. Poison. For a few moments he swayed, too defiant to give in, as his heart pumped fire through his veins. Then his senses failed. He toppled, falling headlong into the bilge alongside the rest.

PART II

1

————

Tar heard before he saw. Birds were cackling and singing, leaves rustling. He smelled tender grass and bawdy, perfumed flowers. He had not heard the stir of leaves in a long while, nor birds among them. He must be dead. Perhaps this was the Atlantean afterlife. Was he in another land, another incarnation? Was this a dream sent by the gods to ease his passage into oblivion?

Then his sight returned to him, and with it a fierce headache, as if the dart had caused his skull to shrink.

He was lying on a smooth, grassy surface. The sky was dawn-pale at the edges, but the belt of stars which Atlantis called the Wake of the Night Ship still split the heavens above, so daylight was yet an hour away. Although his limbs would not respond, he found he could turn his head, and looked about him.

There were indeed trees—and shrubberies, flowerbeds, and lawns. Steep stone hills punctuated the landscape, each with fountains at the top, from which waterfalls spilled down the stone and into reed-fringed streams and pools that wound through the scene, sparkling with starlight. In the distance stood high walls of smooth, burnished metal. It was a man-made place, one of the wealthy families' pleasure gardens.

He was still in Atlantis.

He flexed his limbs and they responded weakly. He had been stripped naked and stank less than before. Someone must have thrown a few buckets of water over him. He propped himself up on an elbow and peered into the thick shadows. There were nine other forms like his own, sprawling on the lawn. They, too, were groaning and stirring from poisoned sleep.

One of these spoke, if only to herself.

"By Dagar's prick! Where the fuck am I?"

Tar pulled himself up onto his knees. He tried to make out the person who had spoken, but the darkness was engulfing. A foreign woman—that was all he knew. He'd never heard of Dagar, nor his prick.

"You," the woman said. "Where is this place?"

She must have been addressing Tar, for none of the others were sufficiently awake to speak to. He tried to reply, but his mouth was foul and his tongue stuck to his teeth. He crawled to a stream that plashed a few feet away and thrust his head into the cold water. He drank deeply. His guts rebelled at the shock and he vomited on the grass. He drank again. It cleared his head and lessened the pain.

"A private garden," he said. "I know not where."

"Atlantis, though?"

"No question of that. What land are you from?"

"The south," she said, and dragged herself to the water, out of striking distance. She splashed her face and drank carefully, and was not sick.

By now another of them was fit to speak. His was a deep, rich voice, although rough from forced sleep. Tar saw a large, powerful set of shoulders, but little else of the man, for he was in the shadow of a cycad palm.

"Look how big this place is," he said, and spat to clear his throat. "We're in the noble quarter of Atlantis. Who can afford their own forest here, but the richest of houses?"

"We must escape," the woman said, and forced herself to her feet. "Climb the walls."

Tar also stood, his head reeling from the effort. The broad-shouldered man did the same, and turned in a circle.

"Look at the stars reflected in the walls—they're perfectly smooth. We won't escape that way."

"There must be a gate! How else came we here?" The woman began stretching and jogging in place to revive her limbs. Tar could see from her silhouette that she was uncommonly tall and thin.

All of the others were conscious now, in various stages, muttering to themselves or each other. Tar approached the woman and she dropped into a fighting stance.

"I am no danger to you," he said.

"Not if I fuck your heart with a knife," she replied, and he stayed where he was.

From everywhere and nowhere came a loud, metallic voice.

"Good morning," it boomed. "Welcome to my garden of delights."

"Who is there!" demanded the broad-shouldered man.

"I am your host," the amplified voice said. "I welcome you to this paradise among paradises. Be warned—all is not as it seems! Here the most perfumed flower may stop your heart, the softest grass may pierce your bowels, and the coolest water burn your flesh. Here in this splendid place, life and death are twin sisters, alike in beauty."

"I know not these others," came a man's voice from farther up the lawns. His accent was that of the people of the eastern shores. "I know only myself. But I have killed more men than any present, and I will kill you, too, coward!"

"You are mistaken," replied their host, and laughed. "On each count. First, there is another here who has killed more men than the rest of you combined. Second, I shall not die by any hand among you. Third, I am no coward, as you will discover—if you live long enough."

Tar was listening closely, hoping for some clue as to the source of the voice. He was also memorizing every word, because he'd heard similar speeches in the fighting pits. Generally, they meant trickery, and preceded slaughter. His mind was working with familiar speed again. He felt the numbness and despair of the chain gang draining out of him, replaced with a fierce desire to survive.

"Release us, you shit-eating toad," the tall woman shouted.

"I shall release one of you," came the voice. "The one who is still alive when the sun sets this coming night."

At these words, the captives moved closer together, forming a loose outward-facing circle. They were all expecting an attack. Their unified instinct to form a defensive ring told him they'd seen combat. Tar looked at the others in the improving light. All manner of bodies, large and small, from many tribes, including a hulking pithecus. They were naked and unarmed.

The voice boomed on.

"The ten of you are the finest killers in all of this island. For my sport, you will hunt each other. Whomever survives —if any of you does—shall be made a freeman of Atlantis. For your trouble you'll receive a fat purse of gold and a ship of your own. I shall not wish you luck, but may your deaths be swift. The game begins now."

The speech ended. Before the last echoes died away, the

ring of captives had split apart. Now they were facing each other, for the threat to them had changed.

"Don't listen to him," said a man with the accents of the land beyond the west. "If we fight each other, we carry his spear for him."

Without any warning, the man nearest to the one who had spoken sprang at his neighbor, and wrenched his neck until the vertebrae crackled.

"That's a good start," said the killer, and hurried as fast as his stiff limbs would carry him into the concealment of a nearby grove of trees.

Seconds later, he screamed. The cry was cut short. Birds complained from above, and a huge, wedge-shaped head was briefly visible against the starlight on the wall, swallowing a shapeless mass from which hung a single arm. Before the thing had finished its feast, the lawns were empty of all figures but the broken-necked corpse.

Eight left.

2

Tar crouched beneath a broad-leafed plant he recognized as harmless from his life on land. His drugged body was reviving, yet far from ready to fight. From his vantage he could see across the lawn where they'd awakened. Behind him was a dense stand of vegetation. He knew the tall woman was somewhere to his left, among the same woods he'd fled into. The others he had not seen disappear.

He did know something about them: There was the pithecus, three times his size. There was one short enough to be a dwarg of the ancient races. If so, he would be powerful but slow. The big-shouldered man was a formidable opponent. It was the woman who concerned him the most. She was built like a praying mantis, no doubt as quick as himself—and fighting women were uncommonly ruthless, even by his standards. If she had been chosen for this game, she was to be feared.

He did not doubt he could kill some of them with his bare hands. But he could never match a pithecus. Their strength was even greater than their size. Their bones could not be cracked, and although like lesser apes they did not fashion things with their hands nor cook their meat, their brains were no less cunning and swift than those of man.

The light was growing. If he wanted to make use of the darkness, he must act swiftly. It was a mistake to waste effort inventing ways to escape from this lushly manicured fighting pit. Their captor would not have made mistakes as simple as that. The only way to survive for long would be to form an alliance with someone among them—and then kill his teammate when the rest were dead.

"Woman," Tar said, hoping he spoke loudly enough for her to hear, and nobody else.

"Keep talking so I can kill you," she replied. She was closer than he'd thought. She must have been stalking toward him.

"There is a stand of spiny whiteflower between us," he said. "If you want to know how quickly it kills, come closer."

"How do you know that, Atlantean?"

"I'm no Atlantean. I was raised in the forest. If you want to survive, join your sword-arm with mine."

"Fuck your ass with your own pecker," she said, but he observed she'd stopped coming toward him.

Tar found the ground at his feet was littered with sticks and branches. The slaves who manicured the garden would undoubtedly toss them out of sight among the trees in order to save effort. He armed himself with a suitable club, heavily knotted at one end.

"Woman," he tried again. "What is your name?"

"Stop talking, you stupid asshole. He'll hear you."

"Then start listening. Do you believe he'll set the survivor free?"

"Of course not."

"Then we must fight together to free ourselves."

"Or until you only have me left to kill."

"We can fight that battle after this one."

As he spoke, a volley of shouts came from beneath the nearest of the stone hills. Then there was a shrill scream and the unmistakable sound of long bones breaking.

Seven left.

"You have never fought a pithecus before," Tar said.

"How the fuck do you know?" the woman snarled.

"Because you're alive—unlike whoever that was."

There was a silence in which Tar thought he could hear her creeping closer. At last she spoke. She hadn't moved.

"I swear by the mast of the Barracuda," she said. "I will fight beside you until the others are dead."

"And I swear the same by Dagar's prick," Tar replied.

To his surprise, he heard her moving to the fringe of the trees. He joined her there. She brandished a crude spear of bamboo, he his club. She looked him up and down.

"That *is* Dagar's prick," she said. "Let us hunt."

THEY STOLE across the lawns and saw none of the others. The sky was pale, the spray of stars fading, and the first hint of color was returning to the world.

"Pithecines hunt in bands," Tar said. "This one is alone, which means he'll put his back to something and kill anyone that crosses his path by ambush."

"So he'll still be there, behind that hill?"

They moved toward the tower of stone. As they came near to it, they discovered the waterfalls were loud enough that their approach would not be heard. Tar whispered.

"I'll go sunwise around. You go the other way. Wait until I have his attention. With that cane spear you can reach his heart from behind. Thrust hard."

"You'd have me get close to him while you stand by? You're as much use as a wooden cunt."

"I speak the pithecine tongue," he replied. "I'll keep him distracted. But act swiftly. I must trust you now."

She made a sound he interpreted to be a laugh, then moved off in the direction he indicated. If she didn't follow his plan, the pithecus would soon relieve him of his arms and legs. The club would do no harm to such a creature.

He could smell the pithecus before he saw him. The waterfalls spilled over ledges in the stone, forming smooth sheets of musical water that reflected the advancing dawn light. He crept from one outcropping to the next until he caught the odor of wet fur. It was not strong—pithecines were fastidiously clean—but Tar had learned as a forest child to detect them by any means, for they considered human flesh a delicacy.

He saw the enormous creature peering in the opposite direction, waiting for another man to come by. He was hidden behind an outcropping, and didn't expect anyone would approach so near at hand.

"Mighty one shakes the ground," Tar said in the language of the pithecines.

It was a common greeting among them, reserved for the strongest.

"Who speaks!"

The pithecus surged up on his bowed legs and thrust his massive head around, but Tar had ducked out of sight. He scrambled up the rocks, hoping he was out of reach, before he replied.

"Man from forest," Tar said. "I am Yunkai."

The words meaning 'man' and 'maker of things' were the same in that language.

"Good marrows, little fish-eater," the pithecus said. "Come and die."

"Mighty one who shakes the ground, how Atlantis?"

"Stolen. Web of men, not spider."

"They caught you in a net? they are cowards. Help me kill them."

"I need no help. Come down and die."

The pithecus had located Tar, and was staring up at him from below. His brow and jaws were monumental, heavy as the vine-wrapped effigies of stone left behind by the vanished First People, deep in the primordial forests.

"We are not enemies," Tar pleaded.

He saw no sign of the woman. She should have been close by now. He was on his own. The hill, he discovered while climbing, was made out of heaped-up boulders. If he could lift one free, he might be able to crack that formidable skull.

The pithecus began to climb. Tar scurried higher, and found the first rays of sun were flashing on the tops of the walls that confined the artificial forest. The birds were at their noisiest. Beyond the walls, Atlantis would be rising for the day, unaware of the deadly game being played in its midst.

The top of the hill was flat, capped in a bronze deck. It formed a lookout that commanded a view all around. Although his attention was on his foe, Tar felt a memory stirring in the back of his mind. He dared to turn his back long enough to look up in the opposite direction, and knew where he was.

Looming over the garden was the palace of House Mannon, its heights gilded by the sun. There was the tower where he'd spent the afternoon with lady Rowana-Ya, and the balcony on which he'd stood. If he survived long enough to find a way into the palace, he might know enough of the place to escape.

The extra moment he'd spent staring at the tower was nearly fatal. The pithecus sprang from below and landed heavily on the deck, snatching at Tar with clawed fingers. They grazed his side but did not catch him. If they did, he would die. Tar ran three steps, leapt, and flung himself over the edge of the hill as he had thrown himself into the sea—without expectation that he would survive. He refused to die by an enemy's hand.

The waterfalls poured down into pools, and he plunged into one of these. The water was warm and fresh, not salt, the pool surprisingly deep, rich with ornamental plants. He scrambled up out of it onto the lawn, knowing the pithecus would be right behind him, and took a fighting stance that would be of no use at all.

Above, he saw the brutal creature at the top of the hill, glaring down at him—but not moving. His eyes were red, his massive features distorted with some agony Tar could not understand. Strangest of all, there were flower petals like pale moths fluttering around his head.

The pithecus fell to his knees. He clutched at his throat, roared with fury, and fell into the pool with a splash that threw half the water over the rocks. There he floated for a few moments, face-down, before sinking as slowly as a ship. The lilies closed ranks around him. He was dead.

Tar looked back to the peak of the hill and saw the woman, rimmed in gold by the rising sun. In her hand was the bamboo spear. There was a branch wedged into the end of it, adorned with tattered white flowers.

"You didn't lie about the spiny whiteflower," she said. "And you make good bait. Let's go kill the others."

Six to go.

3

____

Now that daylight had come, they kept away from the open areas. But as Tar pointed out, half of the vegetation was dangerous in some way. There were few species as swift or strong as whiteflower, but anything that slowed them down would be fatal against a fresh opponent. They ran at a crouch to an area dominated by cycads. There was no undergrowth to conceal a beast.

"Rest here a minute. We're safe against surprise," Tar said when they had concealed themselves among the shaggy trunks.

"Tell me what other dangers we face," his companion said. "I know nothing whatsoever of Atlantis—may LoHaka skull-fuck its ancestors."

He looked her over. Though lean, she was corded with muscle. She was dark of skin, her face and chest decorated with patterned scars like cobblestones. Her hair was cropped short.

"What are you called?" He asked again.

"I'm called the woman with her fist up your mother's ass," she replied.

He couldn't understand why anyone wasted words on insults, the weakest weapon in the world. He tried again.

"I am Tar Yunkai of Men."

"I am Krait Venom Libagoro of Men. Called Krait."

"I'm not calling you that," Tar scoffed. "What is your real name?"

"That *is* my real name. My people are assassins from birth. I'm a pirate. Lost my ship and ended up here."

A pirate. Tar would certainly kill her when the time came. Every pirate in the world was on his list. He had to distract himself before he attacked her there and then. He needed her alive—for now.

"Libagoro…I met one of your people in the fighting-pits," he remembered.

"You're a fucking pit slave? That explains the scars! But why the sores? Your flesh is as pale and rotten as a dead whore's cleft."

He changed the subject.

"I have been in that tower above us, and I know where we are. This is the inner garden of a man called Jaff He-Ah of House Mannon. All you see around us is the work of men. The trees and plants are in bronze pots set into the ground."

"Impossible," Krait said.

"The man-eating beasts must be caged somewhere when they are not required. Otherwise this landscape could not be groomed as it is. These waterfalls are fed from tanks below."

"I don't want a fucking lesson in Atlantean gardening," Krait said.

From the way she gripped her improvised spear, Tar saw she was thinking of killing him.

"Hear me out. What I'm telling you is that we are not standing on the ground, but on a roof. There must be exits and entrances hidden in this place. Do you remember what our captor said?"

"He spoke of bowel-piercing grass, flesh-eating water, and deadly flowers. The last part was true. But we have run through the grass naked, and you didn't die in that fucking pool."

"Look out for water where nothing lives. As for the rest—"

The blaring, disembodied voice once again spoke to the whole of the garden, interrupting Tar's train of thought.

"Six of you remain, and the sun has been up only twenty minutes! But do not idle away the day. If more than one of you lives when the sun-maiden lies down with the sea-god, then all that remain will die."

"Is he making the rules up as he goes along?" Muttered Krait.

"The goddess Ah-Ut-Hur, patron of Atlantis, gave man the gift of making things," their host continued, sounding obscenely pleased with himself. "In her honor, we must furnish you with tools. You have done miracles with sticks and stones and hands and feet. Now let us learn what you can do with weapons."

From a distance came the shout of the big man, their fellow captive:

"Where are they! Answer, you sadistic bastard!"

"The look on your faces is delightful," the voice said, and nothing more.

The big man kept shouting, but there came no response.

"He's over that way near the wall," Krait estimated. "Let's kill him next."

"Wait," Tar said, when she moved to break cover. "Think first and kill after."

"You talk too gods-damned much."

"I've never talked this much in my life. I was told by an old man that every house has a shrine to Ah-Ut Hur, surrounded by water. Like a miniature Atlantis. It can be any size, a cup or a pond. When I was on the balcony up there, I saw a lake in this garden with a pagoda in the middle of it. Somewhere in that direction."

"That doesn't mean the pissing weapons are there."

"Our captor speaks in riddles. Why tell us of Ah-Ut-Hur unless it's a clue?"

"Then we had better hurry the fuck up," Krait said.

4

They went as swiftly as they dared, but Tar insisted they prod the lawns and garden beds before they walked on them. He was now equipped with a long branch, and her the bamboo pole.

"This is just dirt," she said. "We're wasting time When we should be running like gazelles."

Tar knelt down and grabbed a fistful of sod. He peeled it back, revealing a gleaming surface underneath.

"See? Plates of metal. The same as the streets. There could be spring-loaded spikes, pitfalls, pools of crocodiles underneath. This whole garden is a killing machine."

For all her impatience, Krait had been surprised to see the metal beneath the dirt.

"We go as you say," she said. They kept poking the ground in front of them, circling the edge of a dense wood and heading toward the lake.

Their attention was so focused on their path that neither of them saw the kelenken until it was striding toward them across the grass. Tar had seen these giant hunting-birds in the pits. They did not fly, but their hind legs were longer than

Tar was tall, and their beaks could cut a man in half. He'd seen them use these weapons in combat.

"What the fuck is *that?*" shouted Krait.

"Are there no animals in your country? Run."

They risked plunging into the trees. The undergrowth seemed harmless enough, but death thrives in shadows. However, the kelenken had to slow its attack. It was built for sprinting in the open. Here it must pick its way.

In the middle of the wood, with a clearing around it, stood the stump of an enormous tree. It rose up higher than the bird could reach, then ended abruptly as if broken off by a storm. There was a hole in the trunk near the ground, big enough for a man to fit through.

"Get inside!" Krait said, and ran for it.

"No!" Tar shouted, and tripped her with his branch.

She sprawled and came up ready to stab him with her spear. The bird was screeching at them, finding its way with difficulty, but getting closer by the moment.

"That *can't* be a tree," he said. "It was built here, which means it's a trap."

"Oh, fuck off," Krait said, and ran for the splintered giant.

She crouched down to throw herself into the hole in the foot of the stump, but instinct made her twist to the side at the last instant before a huge shape sprang out, pouring from the tree like a snake. For a moment Tar thought it was a mechanism of jointed bronze, for it shone brown like that metal, and was formed of interlocking plates. But beneath it were countless churning legs. It was a millipede.

Without thought, he charged at it and rammed the branch between its slashing fang-tipped mandibles. It snapped the wood to splinters and kept surging toward Krait. Instead of fleeing, she flung herself on its back behind the questing head, gripping its carapace with her knees.

"Flip the fucker over!" she shouted.

Tar had never seen a millipede longer than his own leg. This one was the size of a river crocodile. But it was the insect or the kelenken, so he got close, dancing around its jaws, and rammed the branch among its chittering legs. He pried upward with all of his strength, but the thrashing monster flung him against the dead tree with a hollow clang.

Krait was losing her grip on the millipede. Tar threw himself at it again, and this time he was able to lever it up with the branch. The monster's armored underbelly was exposed. Krait thrust her crude spear under the lower edge of its head, where the belly-plates parted to allow its mandibles to move freely. The shaft plunged in and erupted through its mouth.

The insect twisted and coiled, tearing up soil and bushes. Piercing its head did little to slow it down, but it had forgotten its prey. Krait was thrown aside.

"That won't kill it," she said. It could live for weeks."

A warning croak came from behind them. Tar and Krait scrambled around the back of the artificial stump as the kelenken arrived. It saw easy meat, and began to tear the millipede apart, one of its heavy claws holding the writhing body to the ground while it pried away plates of exoskeleton with its beak, exposing fatty yellow tissue beneath. It feasted, ignoring the insect's clawing legs and twisting body. Thick, green liquid spurted out of the torn flesh.

Forgotten, the fugitive pair stole away through the trees.

Tar was impressed by Krait's skill.

"How do you know to defeat a thing like that?"

"You asked if anything lives where I'm from? Those do."

"There's the lake," Tar said.

The lake was encircled by neat lawns, with woods set back around the whole perimeter. Its surface was smooth, the dawn breeze having died down, and in the center was the decorative pagoda. This stood on a raft of sorts, moored with golden chains. It was two stories tall, each level fringed with eaves of gold. The whole structure was covered in gems. On the near shore of the lake was a shallow boat, but it had sunk up to the gunwales.

"We'll have to swim," said Krait.

Even as she spoke, another of the captives broke from cover. It was the stocky dwarg.

He was bleeding freely from a head wound, but it wasn't serious enough for him even to notice. His body was covered in hair, and he had enormous testicles. The dwarg looked all around him, and did not see the watchers hidden in the bushes.

"Quick," said the dwarg, and beckoned the way he'd come.

A second man emerged. He moved like a stalker of animals and carried a club. Tar hadn't gotten a good look at him before—he was from the northeast, brass-skinned and muscular, marked by the blue tattoo-like stain with which his people were born. It extended from buttocks to shoulders.

Tar had heard that soothsayers could read the blue marks by their shapes, and so learn the future of the bearer.

"We have to get there first," Krait whispered.

"The weapons might not be inside," Tar replied, and lay down flat to watch.

"This boat is scuttled," the dwarg said to his ally. "Can you swim?"

"You can't?" The stalker said.

"Dwargs sink like stones. Bones are too heavy."

"It's lucky we joined forces, then," the stalker said. Without another word, he ran to the shore and dived into the water, so smoothly that the surface hardly stirred. For a long while, he didn't come up. Tar knew this trick. As children they used it it catch shore birds. They'd swim underwater and grab their legs.

Tar was mistaken. The water began to boil halfway across. Then the stalker came surging up, screaming, with smoking red flesh falling from his bones. He thrashed and kicked as if to climb out of the lake and run across it, but soon there wasn't enough left of his muscles to make his limbs move, and he sank retching below, leaving nothing behind but a steaming blotch of pink-tinged foam.

Tar felt his own death brush past him. Had he and Krait tried to swim across, the dwarg and the stalker would be standing at the shore staring at *two* smears of steaming foam.

"No reeds or lilies touching the water. It must be pure acid," Krait said.

The dwarg was staring open-mouthed at the place where his partner had died. He rubbed the back of his neck thoughtfully.

"Of course I can swim, you poor bastard," he said to the lake. "But never go first."

Tar thought this was very wise.

Five to go.

5
____

Tar thought they should kill the dwarg while he was out in the open, but neither of them was armed, even with a stick, and dwargs were immensely strong and hard to kill. He gripped Krait's arm to restrain her, as she was tensing to attack.

"Wait," he whispered. "There must be another way to the pagoda."

"What if he finds it first?"

"Then we kill him when he returns. We have surprise on our side."

None of the other captives had arrived. They might not know of Ah-Ut-Hur, or couldn't find the lake. The dwarg circled the shore, studying the pagoda. As he would eventually pass near their hiding place, Tar indicated they should retreat into the trees and follow him at a distance.

"How can a lake of acid be on the roof of a building?" Krait wanted to know. "It would eat through anything."

"The doctor who repaired our worst wounds in the slave quarters used acid to melt cuts together. That's how this one was done," Tar said, indicating a puckered welt that ran up his left arm.

"What the fuck does that have to do with—"

"He kept the acid in a glass jar. Maybe the lake is lined with glass."

"Fuck. There's no way to it. Even if we could fell a tall tree, it won't reach that pagoda. There are no ropes, and I see no other boat."

"There must be a passage beneath."

They had no idea where to look for a tunnel entrance, but Tar assumed it would be hidden. So the woods made a reasonable place to start. They stayed well behind the dwarg and back from the edge of the trees, one eye behind them in case others arrived. After almost an hour of circling they had found nothing—nor had the dwarg.

"There's isn't so much as a pecker hole here," Krait said. "That fucker who put us here was lying."

"A hole!" Tar said, making the connection. "We saw a fine hole, back there."

"The millipede's nest! How long does it take for one of those huge fowl to fill its belly?"

They moved with infinite care, following their path back through the woods. They bent double most of the way. Then they saw the clearing, and the dead tree. The hunting bird had gone, but the broad-shouldered, deep-voiced man was surveying the scene of the millipede's destruction. Its remains were scattered all over the clearing. The bird had done a thorough job.

The man went down on his haunches, picked up the helmet-like head of the insect, and pulled the remainder of the bamboo shaft from its jaws. He knew the work of human hands. He peered around suspiciously. He strained his thick arms and wrenched a chunk from the head—one of the millipede's poisonous fangs. It was large enough to be a dagger.

Tar and Krait were flat on the ground. If he saw them, the fight would not go well, even two against one.

"If he goes into the hole, we wait. When he comes out, we crush his skull," Tar said.

Even as he spoke, the man stuck his head inside the hole in the tree. He grunted, then tried to fit himself through it.

"He's too fucking big," Krait said.

The man tried to pry the opening wider with his hands, pulling until the muscles in his arms stood out like heavy cables. It defied his strength. He picked up Tar's discarded branch and tried again, prying with all of his weight. The bronze of the tree creaked, but did not give way before the branch snapped.

The big man was undaunted. He scaled the dead tree and examined the top, then circled it a dozen times, much the way the dwarg had circled the lake. Eventually he looked around the wood again—he must have sensed eyes upon him —but seeing nothing, he moved quietly away in the direction of the pagoda.

"Quickly," Tar said, but he said it to Krait's back.

She was already halfway to the tree.

The musty stench of the giant insect filled their nostrils as they moved in single file along the tunnel, Krait in front. The floor of it was littered with broken bones that nipped their bare feet. Animals and men had died there. The tunnel was made of glass, thick and translucent. It had been formed by melting sand around a cylindrical form. No shapes could be made out through it, but a little light penetrated.

"If this cracks," Tar said.

He didn't complete the thought, but remembered the eastern man turning into boiling stew.

The tunnel angled downwards for some distance, then began curving upward, and a glimmer of clean daylight showed them they were close.

They came to a short, steep stair and ascended it into the pagoda. Even by the standards of Atlantis, this was a beautiful and richly-made space, of gold and white metal, gems and marble. It was spacious, but smaller than it appeared from across the lake. There was a heavy altar in the center of the mosaic floor, and carven chairs of red-flamed wood against the walls.

"I see no weapons," Krait said. "Fuck."

"There's another floor above this," Tar said. "But no way up."

There were no stairs or ladders, nor any opening in the polished silver ceiling.

"We could use your prick as a rope."

"I hear voices."

There were window and door openings in each wall, symmetrically arranged, open to the weather. He went to one of the windows and looked out, keeping himself from view. He saw the dwarg first, and then the big man some distance away. They were speaking to each other in an uneasy truce. The big man was gesturing at the woods. Too far to hear their words.

"Look. They join against us," Tar said.

Krait looked out. The two men stepped into the shade of the trees and out of sight.

"Those cocksuckers. The big one needs the dwarg to reach this place. The dwarg needs the big one to watch his back."

"Will the dwarg fit through the opening?"

"You made it out of your mother's gash, and you have a head like a fossilized turd," Krait observed.

"You could just say 'yes'."

"We kill him when he comes up the stairs."

"The same fate waits for us when we return, our hands empty. That big man will be ready at the other end."

"This was your idea," Krait grumbled. "And a stupid fucking idea it was."

Tar ignored her. Criticism was meaningless to him. He measured his hurts in blood alone. Now that they were unobserved, he stepped through the nearest door and examined the exterior of the pagoda. There was a narrow ledge all the way around its base that overhung the lake of acid. It was not floating, but stood on a glass-block foundation shaped to resemble pontoons. The eaves of the roof projected out farther than the ledge—to climb up there would require dangling over the liquid death. Krait joined him and came to the same conclusion.

"The upper floor is open to the air like this one, but one of us shitheads has to climb around the overhang. Over the lake."

"You're a pirate," Tar said. "You must have climbed the rigging often enough."

"You're a jungle monkey. You must climb trees."

He tried a different tack.

"If the weapons are above, the one who climbs up is the first to be armed."

Krait spat on the tiled floor.

"I knew you were a sniveling pussy."

Tar would ordinarily have gone up without hesitation, but the vertiginous horror of life among the pontoons and the constant danger of falling into the sea had made some impression upon him. He hadn't survived that fate, only to be dissolved in an ornamental pond. Then again, he knew what his gods would have to say about his hesitation, if they were inclined to say anything.

"Fuck it," he said, because he knew she would understand the sentiment.

He inched along the ledge to the nearest window opening, levered himself onto the sill, and began to climb.

6

———

The walls were so heavily ornamented that there were excellent hand-holds, and the pagoda was firmly built, so nothing came off when he placed his weight on the sculptured panels and jeweled rivets. He reached the eaves. They were ribbed underneath like the cap of a mushroom, extending out over the acid by about the length of his body.

She was right about his climbing experience, but he had never climbed a tree as smooth as this. After some thought, he thrust his hand between two of the ribs and made a fist, locking it in place. Friction alone would keep him from the fate of the blue-backed man.

He tried his weight on the fist. It held, although the bones in his hand protested at being so compressed. He jammed his other hand into the ribs in the same way and took his weight off one of his feet. He began to sweat profusely. Of all the terrible deaths he'd faced, this one made him most afraid.

"You fucking madman," Krait said from below.

He was gratified to see she was gripping the sill of the window until her knuckles were bloodless. He wasn't terrifying himself alone. He turned his full attention to the ledge over his head. The sweat was making his fists slippery.

He pulled up both of his feet and pushed his toes between the ribs. All of his weight was concentrated on his hands and feet, in the direction opposing their best strength.

He released his first hand and moved it closer to the edge of the roof, locked his fist again, then moved his feet, and finally his other hand. Three times he did this. All the while his strength was fading, his skin growing more slippery.

Almost to the end of the eave, his left foot slipped from between the ribs and his weight shifted suddenly. His other foot came free and he was dangling by his fists like a prisoner chained to a wall. But there were no chains. His guts felt as if they were filled with icy water. His fists were slipping. Krait gasped with horror. She could only watch.

He pulled his feet up, but could not get them wedged in place again. He dangled helplessly over the acid once more, shaking with the effort. There was one way to keep going. He knotted his right fist until it felt as if the tendons would snap, swelling it as much as he could—then released his left hand and swung for the end of the eaves.

As his right hand lost its hold, he caught the sculpted margin of the roof with his left, swung there for a moment, gathering his strength—and drew himself up onto the slope of the roof with both hands, feet scrambling for purchase.

Once he was lying full-length against the roof, he looked over the edge at Krait.

"I'll be right back," he said.

"You'd make a fine fucking sailor," she said.

He scrambled up the bright golden roof and crawled through one of the embrasures of the second floor. The slaves who maintained the pagoda didn't come up there, he saw. There was bird guano on every surface, nests in the roof framing overhead, and a number of crokuls, the small seabirds who filled the Atlantean sky, took wing on his arrival.

There were no weapons in the room. There was nothing in the room but that which the birds had brought. The interior was undecorated and the structural members of plain bronze, pegged together without jewels or gold. There wasn't even a proper floor, only joists and the ceiling below.

So their invisible host had lied, or they had guessed wrong about the hint in his speech. The goddess Ah-Ut-Hur would not provide them with weapons after all. Now Tar had another problem—he had to get down.

KRAIT WAS NOT EXPECTING the ceiling to cave in. A shower of silver panels and bird shit came crashing down, followed by a long bronze beam, and finally Tar, clambering down the beam, one end of which remained upstairs.

"Nothing," he said.

Then he saw what was in Krait's hands, and froze.

"They were inside the frigging altar all along," she said.

She held a cocked springbow at waist height, aimed at his chest. Its six-edged bolt would pass through his flesh and bone like so much smoke. Around her waist was a sword belt, from which hung saber and knife. There were more weapons propped on the wall behind her, well out of Tar's reach.

"Only one bolt, but I won't need two at this distance," she said. "You and the dwarg will die here, then I can kill the big man when he puts his head into the hole at the other end. After that I'll fight my way out of this place."

Tar cursed himself heartily, but he wasn't done yet. While he'd been in the room above, he'd had a moment to think things over.

"Have you noticed," he began, "that we haven't heard from our host in some time? Why is that?"

"Who fucking cares."

"You do, or you'd have shot me by now. He was watching us before. Now he can't see us."

"He's watching us from the palace tower."

"He spoke of the look on our faces, but I've been up there. You can't see faces from that height. He's somewhere down here."

"Where? We've been all over this accursed shit-hole. There are no watchtowers. There are no men on the walls."

"I don't know. But if he can see us up close, then he has to be within killing distance. You are not my enemy, nor am I yours. He is the enemy."

She did not know what to do. He was right. But if he was dead, he wasn't a problem any longer. He could see the struggle in her face.

"You can kill me here. You can kill the two outside. That leaves one more. Maybe you can find him. Then, when he's dead, it's you against whoever is watching us."

"One man with a speaking-trumpet! I don't fear him."

"He made a mistake, do you remember? He spoke of 'us'. He is not alone. The master of that palace commands a garrison of soldiers. I'm certain it's him that brought us here."

She lowered the springbow, if grudgingly.

"Arm yourself," she said. "Why would he do this? I mean this whole contest?"

Tar slung a belt with dagger and sword over his shoulder, augmenting it with a clawed axe, his favorite weapon, thrust into the sash around his waist. Meanwhile he outlined his thinking.

"I know why he'd want me here. I gave his wife something he could not."

"I can guess what *that* was," she said.

"As for you and the others, he wanted the best killers he could find. We've made good sport so far, and if things get dull, he can release monsters into the garden. But now—he can't see us, or he'd have congratulated us on finding the weapons, don't you agree?"

"So far I do."

"That must mean there's no way out at this end of the garden. He wants us where we began, not in a blind spot."

"We have no fucking choice. To get out, we go where he can watch. I'm going to eat his balls."

"Now, let's go back the way we came, kill the others, and then we'll learn how to kill the man who put us here."

7

———

They brought all of the weapons with them, enough for four men. There was no-one at the bronze stump when they emerged.

"They must have heard when I broke through the ceiling," Tar said. "They know we have the advantage now. They'll try to snare us."

"Let's hide these weapons at the edge of the wood," said Krait. "Even the ones we're wearing."

"That's not a good plan," Tar said.

"If they think we're empty-handed, we can lure them in."

That *was* a good plan.

The voice of their host boomed out a few minutes later, when they reached the edge of the lawns where the streams and waterfalls sparkled in the afternoon sun. Time had passed without Tar noticing.

"Five of you remain, and the day wanes," came the voice. "None of you is armed, to the dishonor of Ah-Ut-Hur. I am disappointed. It is time to make the game more interesting. Some new playmates will be introduced, and alterations made to ensure that more of you fall dead. Only one can live."

Tar and Krait tucked all of the weapons but two under a jacka bush, the leaves of which were covered in hairs that would make the skin burn for hours.

"This plant is common along the coasts," Tar said. "They'll avoid it."

They finished disguising the cache with handfuls of leaves. The two weapons they put aside were fighting knives. They emerged from the trees with the knives concealed under their arms, pressed flat against their ribs. Tar went first, probing the lawn in front of them with another length of bamboo.

"Why waste time with that bullshit?"

"He said more of us would fall dead. I think he means for us to literally fall."

"There!"

The man they hadn't yet seen was charging across the grass toward them. He was a shaggy-haired man with the low forehead and sloping chin of the Old People, his feet shaped like hands. While everyone else had been busy, he had fashioned himself a crude atlatl, the lance-throwing stick that had begun mankind's ascent from the beasts.

"Dodge!" shouted Krait, and tumbled like an acrobat. She was faster than Tar, which was a rare thing. The first missile caught Tar's thigh, traveling under the skin without piercing the muscle. The second was already in the air.

Their opponent was a hunter-gatherer. This was how he survived.

Tar rolled and the crudely-carved lance tore through his skin, igniting fierce pain that clouded his mind. He banished it. He'd lost his knife, so he took up the bloody lance. The attacker was gone.

"He disappeared into the fucking ground," Krait said.

"I told you," Tar grunted.

They crept to where the man had disappeared. There was a ragged hole in the turf with a dark void beneath. Tar peeled back a scrap of lawn at the edge of the hole, revealing the sod had been laid over a net of thin wire. The man's weight had torn the net and he'd fallen straight through. He now lay in the bottom of a bronze shaft, his barrel chest pierced by stakes set in the floor. He was still alive, staring up uncomprehendingly.

"Y'et hem. Y'et hem," Tar said, speaking the Old People's language.

The hunter stopped trying to breathe. His eyes closed.

"Four of us left," Tar said.

"What did you say?"

"Hunt the stars."

"You are a sentimental asshole," Krait observed.

Death was his constant companion and he felt he had a responsibility to acknowledge those whom it took on his behalf. Tar honored the dead when he could.

He could feel eyes watching him. He looked carefully at their surroundings. Three of the man-made hills were visible from the lawn, the waterfalls sparkling and burbling. There were also three woods—the one they'd come from, another opposite, and the third between them and the palace. Two sections of the tall copper walls showed between the nearest trees. Somewhere, their host was watching—and the big man and dwarg could not be far away.

"Your leg is bleeding," Krait said.

"I have plenty of blood."

Krait started for the woods they'd come from.

"That fucker said we'd have new playmates," she said. "We should find the densest woods we can, so the whoresons won't be able to charge us."

Tar limped after her, using one of the lances to support his weight.

"I lost my knife," he said.

"I didn't."

"Look for oracle lilies—a tall plant with flowers that look like eyes," he said. "Leaves shaped like galley oars. I saw some before."

"Over there," Krait said. They moved toward a flowerbed overhung by the trees.

Tar borrowed her knife. She took his lance, ready to kill him if he did anything sudden. He cut one of the long flower stalks near the base and tossed the knife back.

"You don't trust anyone, do you," he said.

"Why would I trust you?"

"I don't know." He didn't have the energy to argue.

He was intensely hungry. They should have eaten some of the centipede. He parted the bloody lips of the wound in his leg and let the milk drip from the flower stem into the torn flesh. He sucked air through his teeth when it sank in.

"What does it do?"

The blood stopped running from the wound. It turned black and rubbery.

"It burns like fire," he said. "And clots the blood. Useful for this kind of wound. But dip a blade in it, and it will clot the blood in your enemy's veins."

"I begin to admire this garden."

They moved deeper into the trees. The closer they got to the heart of the wood, the wilder it became, until they were pushing through tangles of lianas and fallen timber. This was not the work of men, but of time. It had been years since anyone groomed this part of the garden.

"Beware," he whispered. "Even the grounds-keeping slaves don't come here. There is danger."

They came upon a clearing with an enormous termite

mound in the center. It looked like a sand castle with many towers, reaching high above their heads, and was the size of a house. The ground was trodden to dust around it, and broad animal paths led away in several directions.

"I don't think there are termites in Atlantis," Krait said.

Tar picked up a stick and threw it. It made a metallic sound when it struck the mound.

"It may be a way underground," he said.

They circled it as silently as shadows. The far side was carved to appear as if it had been scooped out by a giant anteater. Looking closely, they could see a row of bars inside the cavity. A gate.

Even as they watched, the gate began to descend, creaking, into the ground.

"Let's get inside!" Krait said.

"It's not opening for us. This is your chance to climb a tree."

Tar scaled the nearest trunk until he was high up, where the tree forked into smaller branches. He looked down and saw Krait was still on the ground below. The gate clattered to a halt, level with the soil. A low, phlegm-choked growl rumbled out of the passage into the ground.

"Climb!" Tar said.

"I don't know how!"

"Then climb the mound!"

Krait had barely reached the top of the termite chimneys when a massive, flat head emerged from the opening beneath her. It was the thing they'd glimpsed before dawn. Its coat of yellow bristles was striped brown, rising to a crest along its spine. Its jaws were lined with curving orange tusks, its face a mask of protuberances. It was a carnivorous pig, larger than a water buffalo. Tar had seen them in the grasslands to the north of his boyhood forests, but never this close. It stank of musk and shit. Its broad, flat snout sucked at the air. It smelled prey.

Krait was crouching among the the towers atop the mound, only as far from the beast as its body was long. It snuffled at the air with its head up, slender tail flicking.

Tar felt he should do something to distract it from Krait. Eventually she must die, he knew. He could not suffer pirates to live. But for now she was his only ally. The problem was that he had no weapons at all, not even a stick. He could at least get its attention. But he didn't want to shout, or the big man and the dwarg would know where they were.

He stood up in the fork of the tree and urinated down on the giant pig.

It snorted and looked for the source of the stream. When it saw him, it began attacking the tree. The monster wasn't offended at what he had done. It was hungry. He clung to the bark as the pig gnawed and slashed at the trunk, then charged hard against it. The tree shook and swayed. Leaves showered down.

Tar clung to the tree and looked for somewhere to jump. Krait was no longer on top of the termite mound. He couldn't see her anywhere, despite his vantage point. The pig would certainly bring the tree down if it kept tearing at it. He had to come up with some way to escape. He had not died in the pits. He was not dying here.

The pig was even stronger than it looked. The tree abruptly split vertically, then horizontally, and toppled through the grove.

Tar no longer had to think of a way to survive the pig. He had to survive the fall. When the tree toppled into its neighbors, he threw himself off the trunk, crashed into the branches of a smaller tree, and rolled as he hit the ground. It was painful, but he wasn't seriously injured. The pig, however, intended to see that he was. It grunted with satisfaction and charged at him. He ran, leaping over the more dangerous species of undergrowth and plowing straight through the rest.

The beast was right behind him. Nothing was poisonous enough to slow it down. It shattered saplings and bounced off the larger trees, bearing down on him with terrific speed. Tar burst through the fringe of the wood and found himself on the lawns again. If he could get up one of the stone hills, he would survive. He fled straight for the nearest one—and found he was on the same lawn where the hunter-gatherer had died. The ground beneath his feet shook. The animal was close. He could hear its breath whistling through its tusks.

Tar shifted his course toward the trap, sprang across the hole in the sod, and kept going. An ear-splitting squeal followed him, but the pig did not. He looked behind him and saw the animal's hindquarters projecting out of the hole, kicking wildly at the air. After a time, they slowed, then went limp. By then he had reached the hill.

That is where the dwarg was waiting for him.

8

____

The dwarg was clever. He had found the dead pithecus in the pool, and with a scrap of rock or some other improvised tool, had pried out one of the giant's canine fangs. With the root, it was six inches long.

The dwarg lunged for Tar. Tar side-stepped the ponderous attack with ease, but he was exhausted. He'd been drugged, pursued, wounded, had fought a giant millipede and scaled a roof over a lake of acid that day. He had not eaten anything but refuse in more than a month. In a battle of strength, he would not win against this dwarg.

In desperation, he ran.

He wished they had not elected to conceal the weapons. There was the knife on the lawn, but he did not know where it was.

He was running toward the only part of the hellish garden he hadn't yet seen, the end opposite of the lake. The dwarg trotted behind him. Tar had to stop, or he was going to collapse. He bent over with his hands on his knees, gasping for air. The dwarg wouldn't reach him for a few breaths.

"I've seen you now and again this day," the dwarg said. "You worked hard, but you lack stamina. You're pale and tired. I've no quarrel with you, so let me twist your neck. Done in an instant and no suffering at all."

"You're very kind," Tar said.

He ran another short distance. The woods were closing around him, the lawn tapering to a point. At the end, a path led into the trees. He turned to the dwarg, who got closer with every pause.

"I'm going to have to kill you," Tar said. "I have to survive. There's unfinished business before me."

The dwarg was strolling toward him now, scratching his prodigious balls.

"I see from the chafing around your neck and the stripes on your back that you're a slave. Slaves have little pressing business."

"Revenge," Tar said.

"A worthy business is revenge," the dwarg replied. "I am a general of my kingdom, you see. Rismus the Bold. I was captured in battle by nefarious treachery, and sent to rot in a dungeon somewhere on this accursed island. How I came to be *here*, I do not know. It makes a change of scenery, at least."

Tar was surprised to see the distance between them had gotten shorter without him noticing it. He forced himself to jog farther along the lawn, and met the path into the woods.

Rismus kept coming with unstoppable strength and purpose. They were almost to the dead-end corner of the garden, where its wall met the outer wall of the palace grounds. All around were shaggy trees. Tar found the entire landscape in that corner was familiar to him. It was similar to the forests south of Yunkai territory—which meant he couldn't escape through the trees. The woods were under-planted with a type of vine called 'devil's tongue', because its spade-shaped red leaves would blister skin on contact like hot iron. He had seen a boy die of it in the village.

There was an opening in the trees where the walls met. A large pavilion stood in the corner. It was circular, open to the sky, with a plastered wall around it. It was taller than Tar could see over.

Rismus trundled up the path through the trees.

"Be reasonable, lad. You did well, but it's finished."

The path ran to the arched entrance of the pavilion. It was surrounded by flowering vines. The flowers were not a poisonous type. It had to be some cruel trap, he knew, but he had nowhere else to go.

"Let's get this over with. It's tedious," Rismus said.

The dwarg sounded nothing more than irritated. He knew he was going to win, but it was taking too long. He made another lunge. Tar danced away, but clumsily. His reflexes were fading. There was no alternative. He ran into the pavilion.

It was larger than it looked from outside, fifty feet in diameter. However, most of the space was taken up by a circular pond in the center, surrounded by a margin of wood chips. A decorative arched bridge spanned the pond, its axis aligned with the entrance. There was nothing else in the pavilion, no furniture or greenery.

All of this Tar saw at a glance. The dwarg was a few seconds away. If there was danger here, it had to be in the pond. It was filled with cloudy brown liquid, opaque to the eye.

There were no plants in the pond, so the liquid in it could be acid, although it looked different. Tar threw a chip of wood into it. The chip didn't burn or dissolve, but floated on the surface. So the danger in this place wasn't acid. He had hardly finished the thought when the water began to boil furiously around the wood chip. He saw flashes of red and gold as needle-shaped fish tore the chip apart.

Rismus nearly caught him. He'd been distracted by the fish. He felt the clubbed fingers scrape his back as he jolted away. A stupid mistake. He wouldn't have survived it in the arena. But now the dwarg stood between him and the only way out.

"Come, boy. I'm a general of many campaigns. Have you ever seen war?"

"No," Tar said.

He'd seen copies of war in the arena, but never the real thing.

"Let's grapple. We're both unarmed. I'm stronger, but you're faster. It's a fair enough fight."

Tar knew far better than that. Rismus could break his arm in half with one hand. And he'd still have the other hand free.

He had to goad the dwarg into moving away from the entrance.

"When I see your balls," Tar said, "I think you should have a very large cock. But it looks like a thumb."

"You're going to make jokes about my race? This is the best you can do?"

Rismus may have found Tar's effort pathetic, but he'd also come closer. Tar saw somewhere he could lure his opponent that might end the contest. It might also guarantee his death. If he'd had another option, he would have taken it.

The bridge was a high, narrow arch made of bamboo. It was strictly ornamental, lightly built and without railings. It spanned the exact center of the pond, over thirty feet across. He stepped onto it. It didn't collapse. The dwarg was coming in fast.

Tar backed up toward the peak of the arch. The bridge was

about as wide as the dwarg's shoulders, and swayed slightly. Tar was certain Rismus wouldn't follow him onto it.

But he did. His wide, splayed feet seemed almost to adhere themselves to the polished wood. The frame creaked.

"In the pond," Tar said. "Do you know what kind of fish those are?"

The dwarg advanced, arms cocked in a wrestling pose.

"I'm not taking my eyes off you."

"I'll tell you," Tar said. "They're Pikua. In my language that means 'drill'. I grew up in the forest where those—"

Rismus lunged, and Tar skipped nimbly back. His opponent was top-heavy. He saw it in the lunge. The narrow bridge was to his advantage. If he could get the dwarg above him—

"A school of pikua can strip an elephant to its bones in the time it takes to eat a mango," Tar continued. "Do you know how *many* fish are in the pond?"

Tar feinted an attack, which made Rismus lurch backwards—then he overcorrected, rushing at Tar, who scuttled backwards, descending partway down the far side of the bridge.

"A school," Tar said.

His opponent was now at the highest point in the arch. Rismus flicked his eyes from left to right, as Tar had hoped he would. He'd seen the fish. He had to be wondering if what Tar said was true.

"I didn't come here to talk about gods-blasted fish!" Rismus bellowed.

That was the moment Tar had been waiting for. His arms shot out and he caught the dwarg's thick ankles. He pulled like a rower, and the dwarg fell. But he didn't fall into the pond. He caught one of the bridge poles and clung to the structure well above the water.

Now Rismus looked down, and saw there was a swarming

disc of red and gold churning the water directly beneath him. He looked up at the span of the bridge and didn't see the boy.

"Did you fall in?" He was deeply irritated now.

Tar had flattened himself on the deck so the dwarg couldn't see him from below. Now he gripped the far edge of the deck and swung his entire weight over the side opposite, heels first, knees locked. The dwarg hadn't expected this. Tar's feet slammed into his chest.

He had underestimated Rismus' strength—the dwarg kept his fists locked around the bamboo poles that kept him anchored on the bridge.

What Tar *hadn't* underestimated was the strength of the bridge.

The poles tore free of the deck above them. With an ear-splitting yell of fury, the dwarg rode them down in an arc. He slapped the water with his back, sending up a shower of stagnant spray.

Tar pulled himself back up onto the bridge deck, but it was already collapsing. He ran along the deck like a flailing tightrope as the bridge tipped over. He didn't reach the end before it landed on General Rismus. Tar had had to jump wildly for the edge of the pond. He missed it. His legs splashed into the water and his breath was knocked out of him, but he hauled himself out as fast as his muscles would answer.

He slapped his legs in a panic, looking for pikua. None had attached themselves to him—they were fully occupied in the middle of the pond. Tar got to his feet like a groggy boxer, then stumbled around the pond toward the pavilion's entrance. He knew what was coming, and he did not want to see it. Still, he couldn't stop himself from looking back.

Only the briefest of glimpses was enough. Rismus stood up in the wrack of the bridge, tearing at the countless fish that were boring their way toward his vital organs. Rismus' screams didn't stop until Tar was halfway through the devil's tongue wood.

He fell to his knees, completely spent. He remained like that for several minutes, trying to force himself to move.

Two to go.

9

Tar had to face the truth: Of the three survivors, he was in the worst condition. The big man had strength on his side, while Tar's was ebbing away. As for Krait—he admitted to himself that she was a more proficient killer than he, if not more prolific. And the last time he'd seen her, she still had a knife.

He knew what he had to do. From his vantage point he could see across the lawns to the wood where they'd concealed the weapons. If he could reach them, he could still slay both of his opponents. He thought it was most likely that Krait had gone there as soon as he was treed by the pig. In that case, he'd die the moment he came within range of her springbow.

He took another look around. The palace tower and the vast sail above it were golden with the late sun, which was now opposite where it had been that morning. The sun would set before long, and time would be up. He could see the seabirds wheeling over the city beyond the walls, and storm clouds on the distant horizon, purple and gold.

It was beautiful. Motia had died in the midst of a storm,

in darkness and confusion. His silent companion, death, had chosen a peaceful evening for his demise. Then the peace was broken.

"Only two left!" Boomed the host's voice. "Well done! Bets have been won and lost today. Great sums of money have changed hands! Such skilled fighters in such different ways, but in the end, only one may survive."

Tar discovered the voice was coming from a metal horn mounted in a tree. A tube ran down the tree into the ground. The owner of the voice—he was certain it must be the man he had cuckolded, Count Jaff He-Ah—would be at the far end of the speaking-tube, wherever that was.

Tar wished he were a krait himself, in that moment. A real one—a snake. He would crawl down the tube and plunge his fangs into Jaff He-Ah's tongue.

"You have half an hour until the sun lies with the sea. One of you must die by then. The other shall be free. I wish you good fortune, but be swift!"

The echoes faded. Tar worked his way down the hill. The shadows were long and gathering beneath the trees. He saw a pair of shaggy dire wolves slinking across a distant gap in the trees, and heard the screech of the kelenken bird. There would be no need to clean up that day's corpses. They'd be devoured by morning.

Two left.

If Krait still lived, Tar would certainly die. Conversely, if the big man had slain Krait, Tar could still kill him—if he reached the cache of weapons. He must make the attempt. The odds were precisely half for and half against. He'd faced worse.

Tar ran across the grass toward the trees where the weapons could be found. He wasn't worried about pitfalls any more. If he plunged to his death in one of those, so be it.

He did not want to die by a pirate's hand. Better to meet

his fate by mischance. The truth was, he could not hate Krait as he hated pirates in general. She was foul-mouthed and cruel, but she was good in a fight, and clever, and if he had found anything worthwhile about this terrible day, it was the time he'd spent at her side.

He passed the hill where the pithecus had died. He saw the stone, the pools, the waterfalls, and it seemed as if a hundred lifetimes had passed since he stood atop it. The waterfall across the near side of the hill fell so smoothly that he could see the sunset reflected in it like a portal to a better world.

In that moment, he understood. He knew how his tormentors had been watching the action in the garden. It was the only way that made sense. It explained the blind spots, and the watchers' ability to get close to the combatants without being seen.

The realization was followed by an idea, all in one moment. Now that there were only two of them left, Krait would kill him if she could. He was certain of that. But if he could prevail upon her to listen to him, there was a way they might yet escape. It would only succeed if they worked together. The more he considered it, the more possible it seemed. He reached the trees and slipped into the gloom beneath them. Easy hunting in there as the light began to fail —but not for him.

He made it to the bush where they'd concealed the weapons, knelt there to dig them out of the leaf litter, and cursed through his teeth. The weapons were gone. Krait had survived, the big man had died, and Tar had come straight to the place she was expecting. She, too, had a plan. Without even looking around, he raised his hands over his head, still on his knees.

"Hear me out once more," he said.

"You talk too fucking much," said Krait.

She stepped from behind a tree. Her sword belt was buckled on again. She was covered in blood—so much that it could not all have been hers. Otherwise she wouldn't be standing. The big man must have died hard. She was aiming the springbow at Tar's belly.

"I have an idea, but it requires that I trust you completely," he said.

"By Grypka's magical nutsack, you are the biggest fuckwit in all the world."

"I think you trust me, though."

"I don't trust you at all. Which is more than I trust most people."

She brought the bow to her cheek. Tar rushed to finish his proposition before she killed him.

"I know the secret of this place, and how to escape. But it needs both of us to work."

She didn't shoot, so he carried on.

"You saw the entrance to the pig's cage in that termite mound. It's built for big animals. The bars on the gate are spaced so far apart a man—or woman—could easily slip through."

She lowered the bow.

"I saw more than that, dickhead. I went down there to escape that pig. There were fifty big cages knee-deep in dung, but no animals. They must be up here with us. There's a door at the back leading somewhere else, but it was locked and barred."

"That will lead to the palace," Tar said.

"No shit. Then there was a huge crash above, so I came back up and saw your tree had fallen—and you and the pig were gone. I assumed it ate you."

"I assumed you'd run away while the pig tore my tree apart."

She flared with anger and raised the bow again.

"Of *course* you fucking did. You think you're better than me, always doing the right thing. Fuck that. I don't need you. I don't owe you anything. You can stick your honor or rectitude or decency or whatever the fuck it is straight up your ass, and then ride it to hell."

"Noted," Tar said.

"So what is this brilliant idea of yours?"

At least she was listening. Hours earlier she'd have killed him without a second thought. If his plan made sense to her, she might not kill him at all. The flaw in it was as he said: He had to trust her with his life.

It was getting very dark, the sunlight nearly at the top of the mast, fading like the embers of a fire. Stars were showing through the purple-blue veil of the sky. There were only minutes left.

He told her his plan.

10

The Golden Prince burst out of the treeline. He gripped a heavy stick, but was limping badly. The exhaustion he'd shown before had finally taken over. He was running on willpower alone. A few moments later, the naked pirate woman appeared behind him, a jagged, lance-length splinter of wood in her hands.

He turned to face her, and they circled each other like lions. He swiped and missed. Then he ran toward the hill where he'd killed the pithecus. He was seeking the high ground. The woman only had to trot to keep up.

The Golden Prince tried, but he couldn't muster the resources to climb. He slid down the rocks, then turned his back to the waterfall to make a desperate last stand. The woman stalked closer, wary of his club, but confident of the outcome. Her face was twisted with anticipation.

He swung wildly. She got in under the swing, thrust upward, twisted her weapon, and the pit-fighter cried out.

"We had a deal," he gasped, clutching his belly. He staggered backwards, then fell into the pool behind him. The waterfall spilled down on his body like a benediction from the gods.

The pirate tossed her improvised spear aside.

"I win. Now free me," she shouted to the world in general.

"Congratulations," the voice said. "You did it, with only moments to spare—see, the sun now fades from the top of the mast. You have triumphed."

"What a fucking treat," Krait said.

"I owe you freedom and a ship, as I recall. Did I offer you gold as well? I can't recall. To tell the truth, I was making it up as I went along."

"You offered me your word."

"The truth is, I offered you a reason to fight, nothing more. It's a pity none of you found the weapons, because the best part of the game has only just begun."

"I *won*, you sick fuck! Let me free!"

"You won a title. You're now the best fighter in Atlantis."

"Release me, or I'll fuck you in the eye socket with your own prick," she said.

The host laughed. It sounded harsh through the speaking-tubes, like a hammer on sheet brass.

"You don't know whom you outlived today, do you. A great Dwarg general. Never lost a battle. Two of the finest assassins ever born—they've killed kings and queens. The pithecus was an executioner, the primitive hunter who stalked the last of the giant reptiles. Every one of your opponents had a genius for death. Do you know who that last one was?"

"Tell me, and then let me the fuck out of here."

She was turning in circles, as if looking for the source of the voice. She never looked at the waterfall.

"He was the Golden Prince," the host continued. "You may not have heard of him, as this is your first visit to our glorious nation. He was the finest pit fighter in the history of Atlantis. In combat he killed hundreds—maybe thousands, I have no idea. If he hadn't tried to escape, he'd still be doing it. I couldn't let such talent go to waste, rotting away in a chain gang under the island."

Krait was growing desperate.

"Fuck the ship. Fuck the gold. Let me out of your pisshole of a garden and I won't come back to kill you."

"My money was on the Golden Prince, you know. I lost a small fortune today. I can still win it back, though. The one who kills you tonight wins all. I only have to make sure it's me."

"I'm not a fucking animal!"

"No! You're far, far more than that. Hunting is the finest sport in all the world, only limited by the quality of the prey. Men make for the finest hunt, the deadlier the better. And you have proven you're the deadliest man alive. Or woman, as it happens."

Krait backed away from the hill. The voice spoke once more, by which time she was running full-tilt into the darkness that had swallowed up the pleasure garden.

"You have fifteen minutes, and then the hunt begins. Good luck to you, and better luck to us."

A DEAFENING HORN SOUNDED A SINGLE, sustained note. Huge silhouettes began to lope across the lawns. There followed much noise in the woods, of animals crashing through the undergrowth, panting and growling, and tree-birds safely above the fray, protesting at the disturbance of their sleep. After a time the night grew still again. Insects took up their nocturnal symphony.

The waterfalls ceased flowing.

Behind them were dripping, algae-stained voids, separated from the garden by cl0th of Atlantis supported by bars of rustless Atlantean steel. Lamps were lit within, revealing plastered walls and floors strewn with rich tapestries, comfortable chairs and couches. The remains of a fine meal were scattered over a long table of real wood, the most valuable material in Atlantis. House-slaves began tidying up, indifferent to their strange surroundings.

The artificial hill was an observatory, from which there were views of the gardens in every direction. Each of the viewing positions was concealed by a waterfall. Every one of the hills was so equipped, as could be seen now that the water pumps had stopped their work for the day.

A cunningly-concealed door, clad in solid stone so that it appeared to be part of the hill, swung open on heavy hinges. Torchlight stretched out of the opening across the grass. Six well-armed men in gleaming plate and mail stepped out of the hill and into the night. They were followed by thirty well-armed beaters equipped with smoking torches and slender hunting spears.

The man in front wore the three angler-fish of House Mannon on his breastplate. He was Count Jaff He-Ah, and when he spoke, it was with a miniature version of the voice that had taunted the combatants all day.

"My friends," he said to his companions, "this may be the finest hunt we've ever enjoyed.

"When it is over, the world will be a safer place, for we will have rid it of ten of the most brutal vermin with which it has been plagued. The traps beneath the sod have all been sealed and the beasts are safely caged. May the gods bless us —and especially me. Did I say fifteen minutes or ten? No matter, let the hunt begin."

There was shaking of hands and slapping of backs among the armored men. The last of the beaters, their foreman, closed the hidden door behind him and locked it with a key

as large as his hand. Then the entire hunting party followed
Krait's path into the darkness.

Tar waited until they were gone, then dragged himself out
of the pond. He was shivering uncontrollably, having
remained in the water much longer than he'd anticipated.
None of the men had spared him a glance, he was relieved to
see. Krait's performance had been flawless—almost too good.
She had torn his skin when she pretended to gut him. In the
instant in which she made the thrust, Tar thought she actually meant to kill him, but she was true to their purpose.
After that, he only had to play dead.

His theory about the waterfalls had proved correct. From
behind the thin screens of water, their captors watched
events unfold in the gardens. No doubt they took underground passages from hill to hill, to follow the fighters'
progress. There would be a way into the palace from inside
the hill—and unlike the dungeon in which the animals were
kept, it was unlikely to be barred to access. None of them had
any reason to expect there was another fighter still alive,
stalking them from behind even as they hunted their quarry.

Tar stole into the darkness, heading for the weapons
cache, where Krait had agreed to leave them once more.

Let the hunt begin.

Krait was waiting for Tar under the trees, armed and
ready. She helped him equip himself in the darkness. He
hefted the fine hawk-axe in his hand and gave his saber an
experimental flourish to check its balance. The goddess Ah-
Ut-Hur had indeed blessed the survivors of the day—these
were better weapons than he'd had in the fighting pits.

They spoke in low whispers.

"It's as I thought," Tar said. "There are rooms behind the
waterfalls, and they connect with the palace. We can't get in
through the openings, but there's a hidden door, and I know
where it is."

"The beasts all ran off when that fucking horn sounded," Krait said. "I think it's feeding time. They were going in the direction of the termite mound."

"That will save us some trouble."

"True. But listen—while I was underground, I found the mechanism that opens and closes all of the cages. So if we want to make things more interesting, I know how."

Tar observed she hadn't used any obscenities. Her mind must have been too focused on the task before them to spare any extra words.

"It's time," he said.

They thrust out their hands and clasped each other's wrists in the way of soldiers. He remembered the words he'd repeated countless times with his fellow slaves before they went into the pits to die. They suited this moment better than any others.

"Die with a red blade," he said.

They sprinted into the darkness together. Tar's wolf-lean soul had starved for vengeance. This night, it would feast.

11

———————

The procession of torches wound its way through the sinuous lawns, led by the six armored men. It came to the southernmost end of the gardens, farthest from the deadly lake. Count Jaff raised his hand to call a halt.

"We begin here, and tighten the noose until the sea-witch hangs. She won't show herself in the open. Beaters! Clear these woods!"

The thirty spearmen, soldiers recruited for the task, fanned out and began marching through the undergrowth. They were clad for the night's work. They wore thigh-length boots, long gauntlets, and skirted Arming-coats of rhinoceros hide, girdled with short sword, hunting-horn, and dagger. On their heads were studded helms with aventails of padded Atlantean mail that hung to their shoulders. No poisoned thorn or sap would reach their flesh.

The torchlight made the trees crowded around them appear to dance. They sang a marching-song so that each man knew where his fellows were, to keep their line neatly spaced. Their foreman, the man with the keys, sang the first verse, the others sang the next, and on it went:

THE TIGER *with its coat of red*
  Shall stalk these woods no more
  We pierce the bushes with our spears
  And drive the beast before.

WE FOUND *a rabbit in the grass*
  We found a nesting bird
  Do we kill them one and all?
  Oh master give the word.

BLUNT *not your blades on lesser prey*
  The helpless and the weak
  Today we keep our metal bright
  For tiger's blood we seek.

THERE WERE DOZENS OF VERSES, each naming different animals, always to be rejected. Only the tiger would do.

There were two tigers that night, glad of the singing and torchlight. It made their targets easy to find.

The first beater to die was on the end of the line nearest the high wall of the garden. He was chanting and thrusting his spear into the undergrowth, and then he was silent—but his torch did not fall. None missed his voice. The short man to his right presumed he was still there, for the firelight glinted upon his studded helm.

When the torch came closer, the short man muttered a warning.

"Urb-Tah! You stray. Get back to your place."

Tar muttered no warning, and the short man died next. His torch didn't fall, either.

COUNT JAFF and his plate-armored fellows loitered behind. The night was young. There wouldn't be any proper hunting until the pirate was trapped at the far end of the garden.

His companions were his cousin, Count Er of House Dolphin; Count Liad of House Erito, of equal rank to both, although senior in the hierarchy; General Te-Wa-Ut, called the Fang of Atlantis; Admiral Sea-Eagle, who commanded the fleet; and finally Prince Toba-Ke Mobi, a landsman whose nation was a vassal state to Atlantis, providing it with slaves and metals. Although the prince was highest-ranked in the party, he was of lower status, as he was not a born Atlantean.

It was the prince who first observed something was wrong.

"I say, Count Jaff. Aren't there thirty men with us?"

He was feeling nerves, for he had never hunted in this garden, and had not hunted man. The rest never missed an opportunity, be the quarry man or beast.

"Thirty fine men. Only my most loyal soldiers get this honor."

"I count twenty-six torches."

There was a brief pause as the others made their own calculations.

"I count twenty-five," said General Te-Wa-Ut, surprised.

"They'll have gone for a piss," Count Jaff said. "The best men are but men, after all."

"Twenty-four," Count Liad said. "The one at the end just went out. And so did another!"

"Are they drunk?" said Count Er.

He thought Count Jaff's men lacked discipline. Of his own garrison he was very proud.

"Something's wrong," the prince said.

Something was *very* wrong. For now the woods were on fire.

Tar and Krait, the tigers, had begun killing their way down the line of beaters from opposite ends. When the guests counted twenty-four torches, two of those were in the hands of the tigers. Only twenty-two of Count Jaff's men remained alive. The beaters had begun to realize the problem before their masters, for the number of their singing voices had dwindled.

Their killers, meanwhile, had been dousing torches by shoving them into the soil. Some of these had found fuel of leaves and sticks, and the blaze swiftly grew. Killing by stealth would no longer be possible, but the tigers had anticipated that.

A desperate scream split the night and one of the beaters ran blindly through the woods, engulfed in flames, spreading the fire as he went. He reached the lawn on the far side of the trees before he fell.

"You said she was the finest killer in all the world," said Count Er. "For once we agree on something."

He was more amused than alarmed at this disaster. Count Jaff was red-faced inside his helm.

"I'll have the fools flogged for this! Never happened before."

The prince was not so confident as Count Er.

"She can't have gotten men on both ends of the line at once," he said.

Admiral Sea-Eagle snorted with disgust.

"This sort of thing doesn't happen on the ocean. These ridiculous gardens! You can't see a proper distance, and you've got to walk everywhere. If the Gods had wanted men to walk, they wouldn't have given us ships."

"With respect, Count," said General Te-Wa-Ut, "I suggest you gather your beaters. They're scattering to the winds."

Count Jaff was too angry for words, so he lifted his golden horn to his lips and blew three sharp notes.

TAR AND KRAIT met at their assigned rendezvous, at the gate in the the termite mound. At first they did not speak, but caught their breath. They busied themselves tightening the straps on their armor and arranging their weapons, for they had equipped themselves on the fly from the men they killed. Tar gave up in disgust.

"I can't see a damned thing," Tar said.

"Don't look straight at what you want to see. Look next to it. You'll see the outlines."

"It works. How do you know that?"

"I told you earlier. Assassins from birth. My people see in the dark, swim underwater for great distances, and turn invisible. I was never good at turning invisible, so I became a pirate instead."

Tar didn't want to discuss her career. He still didn't know what to do about it.

"You killed more men than me," he said.

"Are we counting? Then I claim five. I set the last prick-stain on fire," she said. "Did you see that? Amazing."

"Only three for me," Tar admitted. "Got delayed. I thought I'd stepped in a poisonous sponge-fungus, which grow in woods like this. You die on the spot and the fungus eats your corpse. But it was the remains of the man who broke the first neck this morning. I stepped on his lungs."

"That giant pig got him."

The three notes from Count Jaff's horn reverberated off the walls of the garden.

"Do you know the meaning of that horn?" he asked. He knew nothing of such things.

"They're recalling their men."

"Then they're going to talk about strategy. Let us hear what they have to say," Tar said.

THE LINE of beaters had broken apart as soon as the fires broke out, and had fled onto the lawns in every direction to escape the growing inferno. Recalled by the horn, the bewildered survivors returned to their master, one or two at a time. They weren't sure what had happened. Only a dozen of the beaters still held torches. The rest had dropped theirs. Count Jaff was furious.

"You have embarrassed me in front of great company! There will be consequences for this."

The foreman stepped out of rank and prostrated himself on the grass at his master's feet.

"Your Glory, I do not know what happened."

"Your career has ended and you're going to drop a caste. That's what happened," Count Jaff snarled.

General Te-Wa-Ut strode forward, bellowing in his most soldierly voice as if there were a thousand men in front of him, not twenty-two.

"If any of you can tell us what occurred, then speak!"

Two of the beaters fell to their knees.

"I saw the pirate woman," the first one said. "She was wearing our armor and carried a torch. Then she was gone."

"And you?" the general barked at the second man.

"I was on the other end. I thought it was one of us at first, helmet and all, but he was setting the trees alight."

A third man fell to his knees.

"I saw the same. One of us, but he put his torch to the bushes."

The general turned to Count Jaff with slow majesty, like the rudders that steered Atlantis.

"We saw every one of the killers die, except the easterner with the blue back. We know he's dead because the dwarg told the giant about it within our hearing."

Count Jaff was trying to contain more fury than his face could conceal.

"I do not like the inference you're making, General."

It's no inference, Count Jaff. The woman is the lone survivor of the selection process. Therefore, one of your own men has turned against you."

12

―――――

Count Er could not have been more pleased by this turn of events. As noble cousins, he and Count Jaffa had been companions since they were infants. Consequently, they loathed each other.

"Dear cousin, we should have used *my* men. I did mention it."

Count Jaffa stamped the ground, determined not to be provoked. He addressed his men through gritted teeth.

"Every one of those trees cost me more gold than a man can carry. Those flowers and bushes I have collected for decades, from every limb of the compass. If you would escape the chain gangs beneath our feet, you'll put out that fire and find me the pirate."

"These men need orders, not demands," General Te-Wa-Ut interjected. "With apologies, great Count Jaff."

"Do what you can with them," Count Jaff grumbled.

The general thrust out his hand and divided the remaining beaters into three parties.

"You there! Mount the hills and keep watch. if you see anything or anyone doing the unexpected, sound one blast on your horn. You lot: Organize the slaves to carry water from the pools and put out that blaze. The rest of you, come with us."

"None of this would have happened at sea," the admiral lamented.

The foreman spoke meekly.

"What of me, Great General, Fang of Atlantis?" he was still stretched out on the grass at Count Jaff's feet.

The general looked at the man with less contempt than his master did, but still a great deal of it.

"You fetch the rest of the palace garrison. I want a hundred good swords in this garden, and I want them now."

Count Liad was a cold man, tall and hard of limb, older than the others. He had hunted every animal worth the killing, and loved nothing more than to drown his weapons in dangerous blood. As he watched the beaters rush off to their tasks, he was at last moved to speak.

"My friends. I don't believe this is an embarrassment at all. No, this is indeed the finest hunt I've ever joined, for our prey shows her us that she is indeed formidable. My appetite is whetted. I think I'll set out to win this most extraordinary prize, and we shall feast on her flesh tomorrow. Which of you shall join me? Prince Toba-Ke-Mobi? Admiral? General?"

"I'd be honored," said Count Er, stung that he had not been invited by name.

"Then good hunting," said Count Liad to the others.

He and Count Er went into the night, silhouetted against the fire at first, then painted red by its light, and finally merging into the deep darkness beyond.

THE GENERAL WAS A SKILLED LEADER, but he dealt in matters of platoons and armies, not solitary fighters. Individual soldiers were for running errands. When he sent the foreman off to fetch more soldiers, he sent him to his death.

The foreman was far more frightened of his master than anything else at that moment, and had forgotten there was a killer somewhere in the shadows.

For his part, as soon as Tar had heard the general shout out exactly where to intercept the key, he had sprinted to the stone hill with the door concealed in it. Tar knew the hills were useful for long views. What happened directly beneath could not be seen. The watchman who now stood on top of it was staring in the direction of the fire.

Tar approached from the opposite side without any difficulty at all, and once he was in the shadow of the hill, he was out of the watchman's sight. He made his way around until he was close to the hidden doorway—moments ahead of the foreman.

He waited until the foreman had fitted the key into the lock, for he didn't know where to find the disguised keyhole. The instant the key was in, he sprang out of his hiding-place —the same niche in which the pithecus had concealed himself.

The foreman drew his sword, but they never crossed blades. Tar struck so fast the man's hand was still gripping his weapon when it fell to the grass. The foreman stared in horror at the stump of his wrist.

"Is that the master key?" Tar asked him. "Does it open all doors?"

The foreman nodded, lost in shock. Then he fainted and fell to the grass. Tar turned the key and pulled the heavy, irregularly-shaped door open. He understood why the key had to be so large. It was also the door handle. He dragged the foreman through the opening, moving swiftly so that he would not be discovered by the beaters fighting the fire. The watchman above had not seen or heard anything.

Inside, Tar drew the axe from his belt. He had to keep well out of sight, because the lamps were burning brightly and much of the hill's interior could be seen from outside through the large viewing ports.

The first thing he noticed was the smell. A nauseous, sweet smell like rotten fruit, overlaid with flowers.

Heptumu.

A curtain stirred in the wall opposite. He crouched low to avoid being seen and yanked the curtain open. There was a flight of steps downward. At the bottom he saw a corridor leading toward the palace, and the stink of his old master was heavier still. He heard distant footfalls echoing against the metal walls. His first instinct was to follow the odor, find Heptumu, and hack him to pieces. He wanted nothing more.

But Krait was alone in the killing garden. She was not a mêlée fighter like Tar. She fought by stealth. If enough men came at her at once, she would die.

He owed her nothing. She owed him nothing. He wanted vengeance against Heptumu so much it burned in his guts. If she found the door in the hill standing open, she could escape on her own. He wasn't obligated to stand by her any longer. What had she said to him? That he had some kind of self-righteous moral code? A stupid idea. He resented it. Yet —it might be that she was right.

Seething with fury, he slipped outside and closed the hidden door behind him. He used the tip of his sword to mark the position of the keyhole, then tucked the key into his armor and returned to the fight. Vengeance against Heptumu would have to come in the future—or never at all. It was up to the gods, and Tar's gods didn't care about his desires.

13

———

Count Liad and Count Er moved quietly between the stands of trees, keeping to the deepest darkness at the foot of the perimeter wall. Count Liad explained his plan as they went.

"They'll drive her toward the shrine of Ah-Ut-Hur. If we're there to meet her, then the killing blow is ours. We'll be at her back when she expects us in front."

They reached the lake without incident and began their vigil.

Count Jaff was mad with the sting of humiliation. His prized garden of dangers was badly damaged and he'd lost a number of men. Even so, none of that mattered as much as being made to look ridiculous.

He was striding across the broadest part of the lawns with the general, the admiral, and the prince. They had six beaters with them. They were in no danger, because the woman had no long-range weapons. He and his guests were armed with springbows. She'd be dead before she got within thirty paces of them, as long as they stayed in the open.

The whole of the garden was lit to some degree by the fire, but the farther they got from the blaze, the darker the shadows became, the firelight serving no purpose at a distance but to dazzle the eye.

"Should we leave the garden, Count Jaff?" asked the prince.

"Why would we do that?"

"Then you can release your menagerie. The beasts will find her by smell. We could search all night with our poor senses."

"There's no sport in that—and I want justice."

Admiral Sea-Eagle spoke up.

"In ocean battles, we chum the water. Spill animal guts over the sides of the ships. The hunting fish smell the blood, and anyone that goes overboard is torn to pieces. Eliminates the enemy swimming to our vessels. Also prevents desertion."

"That's a different circumstance," said General Te-Wa-Ut.

He had a low opinion of the admiral. To him, there was little glory in fighting on water, for all Atlanteans were born upon the water. It was their native soil, so to speak. It was far more valorous to fight on unfamiliar land, and conquer the foe on their own turf.

"I don't mean to say we throw guts about the lawns," the admiral said. "My thinking is that we can drive the woman where we want if she cannot stay where she is."

"I'm not setting fire to any more of my landscaping, if that's what you mean," objected Count Jaffa.

"I was thinking of your tanks of fresh water," the admiral said. "You boasted of a million gallons beneath the palace. I know the displacement of that. it's enough to flood this entire enclosure as deep as a man is tall, and the walls are more than strong enough to hold it in."

"With the deepest respect, Admiral," said Prince Toba-Ke-Mobi, "There is a lake of acid here. Flood it, and it will kill everything."

"We must wait for those reinforcements," the general barked. "Count Jaffa, I sent orders for one hundred of your men. Yet they are not here."

"I'll see to it myself," Count Jaffa said. "You two come with me."

He turned heel and went back the way they'd come, accompanied by the beaters he'd addressed. The smoke from the fire was filling the garden like a fog by now. The count saw a long line of slaves passing leather buckets from one to another, emptying the water features to extinguish the fire. His own men had fetched a two-man siphon pump and a long hose of whale gut, and were spraying the flames with that. The effort seemed only to be adding steam to the smoke.

"I see her," hissed one of the beaters. "Look!"

He pointed out a figure with its back to them, peering around the trunk of a tree in the grove that concealed the entrance to the animal cages. It was watching the attempt to put out the fire, which was across the lawn in the next stand of trees.

"You'll have the foreman's job after I knock him down to Dugra status," said Count Jaff to the beater.

Then he spoke to both of them: "I don't care which of us kills her. If you get the chance, do it, and I'll buy you a fine slave. But you will tell the others I killed her. Understood? We'll take her from three sides. I'll take the first shot, then we come in fast."

The two beaters bowed deeply and said nothing. They

knew their master's word often changed with his mood, but the offer of a slave was highly inspiring. With weapons drawn, they headed toward their quarry.

TAR DIDN'T KNOW how much time had gone by since he left Krait's side. The plan they had devised was short on details. She would kill everyone she could, and he would prepare their escape.

She claimed to lack the skill of invisibility prized in her tribe, but he didn't bother looking for her. She was too invisible for him. He circled around the perimeter of the garden, keeping to the darkest shadows, until he was near to the woods that concealed the termite mound.

Three of the plate-armored men stood on the lawn between him and his objective, with six beaters at their back. He wanted to attack them at once—his thirst for blood was driving him mad—but there were three springbows among the men. He'd never get close enough. His opportunity would only come if they needed to reload.

COUNT JAFF CREPT through the rustling darkness of the undergrowth, then found a perfect spot from which to shoot. He was a good marksman, if not as good as Count Liad. He braced his leg against a log to steady himself and sighted down the bolt in his weapon. The bow twanged. The bolt thudded into the woman hiding behind the tree. Straight through her head, so that her body didn't even fall. She was pinned to the tree.

In case she *wasn't* dead, however, he joined the charge he'd planned with the beaters. His men came in from left and right, the count from behind, swords ready.

They never completed the attack, but stopped and stared at the corpse.

"That's a *man*," said the beater who had been promoted to foreman.

"Already stuck to the tree," the other said.

It was true. The man was one of Count Jaffa's soldiers. Someone had nailed him to the tree with another bolt. From its decoration, it was the one from the shrine of Ah-Ut-Hur.

The count's first reaction was rage at having been tricked once again. Then fear got the better of him. This had to be a trap. She'd lured them to this place. He spun around, sword up. There was no-one behind him. He reloaded and cocked his springbow by feel, never taking his eyes off his surroundings. He strained to see into the shadows between the fire-lit trunks.

"She must be close," he said. "Be wary, men."

His men didn't respond.

He spared a glance over his shoulder. They were gone. Icy-cold panic rose up in his chest like a sudden tide. She must be within arm's reach of him, yet he could not see her. He backed himself against the tree and stumbled over the corpse of his new foreman, whose head had been mostly separated from his body. He tried to shout for help, but his throat had gone dry. He coughed until his eyes were streaming and his mouth tasted of smoke and bile.

There was a knife-point touching the crease in his skin where jaw met throat—right behind the silken knot that secured his helm.

She whispered in his ear.

"You are the shittiest hunter in the world," she said. "You're such a shitty hunter, I was crouching right there at your feet. You leaned on me to steady your aim."

"Please. I'm worth more to you alive," Count Jaff croaked. "I can make you rich beyond your dreams."

"Then I'll regret this for the rest of my fucking life."

She drove the blade up through his tongue, his palate, his sinuses, and finally his brain.

14

———

"Have a drink," said Count Liad.

He offered a fish-shaped silver flask to Count Er. They sat comfortably against the far wall of the garden, springbows in their laps. Their view of the gardens was excellent and none could approach them unseen. The firelight was reflected in the uncannily smooth surface of the deadly lake. It sparkled in myriad colors through the jewels that encrusted the pagoda and turned its golden roof to copper.

Count Er took a swallow and gasped.

"What is that, if not liquid fire?"

"Thrice-distilled *harukh*. It's made from trees in the cold north, where the rain turns to snow for half the year. The trees have pins instead of leaves, I'm told, and bleed golden blood."

"Golden blood? That's what they say of kings."

"I never saw the forests myself. I was in the grasslands below them. Killed a mammoth with tusks as long as its body, and a rhinoceros covered in red curls with a horn so large I had it carved into a chair."

Count Liad was not boasting. He was merely reminiscing.

"Surely this reed-thin woman is no more dangerous than those formidable beasts?"

"Worm asps are no larger than your little finger, yet so deadly Count Jaff may not release them into the garden. They are impossible to see until it's too late. I think our prey is much like that."

"She can't reach us here by stealth."

"I devoutly hope she finds a way. It will make the kill more challenging. Do you want to see something extraordinary, Count Er?"

They rose and went down the grassy swale to the edge of the lake, which was rimmed with sand-glass. Count Liad drained the last of the liquor from his flask.

"It is difficult to imagine the power in this tranquil pool without a demonstration."

He tossed the bright flask into the lake. In an instant, the silver turned black. Then green flames shot up from it, the metal turned to flakes of white like burnt leaves, and it was gone.

"That is life, is it not, Count Er? We are but silver baubles, brilliant for a moment, then consumed."

"A nasty way to die," said Count Er.

"One of the worst. Your cousin Count Jaff offered me your hunting-grounds in Khatha if I threw you in alive," said Count Liad. "Luckily, I am not so cruel as that."

He cut his companion's throat with a powerful stroke of his skinning-razor.

Count Er fell to his knees, clawing at the foaming, frog-mouthed wound. His blood spewed over the acid shore and made it boil.

Then he fell dead, splashing halfway into the lake. The acid devoured him like swarming crocodiles. Count Liam pushed the rest of the corpse in with the toe of his boot.

"So many lives lost to that pirate woman," he said. "What a tragic night."

He went back up the swale and resumed his vigil against the wall.

15

———

"General, where are those men?"

The prince was frightened now. He fervently wished his first man-hunt hadn't involved such a formidable opponent.

General Te-Wa-Ut turned to look at the chaotic scene behind them. It was like watching a play. They were clustered on the quiet grass, untouched by confusion, while the actors rushed about on the burning stage.

"That little foreman of Count Jaff's must have run away. I don't think he raised the alarm. No matter. The garrison will have seen the fire by now. Listen! That's a battering-ram. I know and love the sound. They'll soon be here."

The admiral was not so confident.

"Why a battering-ram? There's a door."

The general was correct. Count Jaff's entire garrison had mobilized when they saw the smoke and flames rising above the garden walls. They had swarmed down the underground corridors and reached the artificial hills—but none of them had the master key that opened the door into the garden. There were only four such keys. Count Jaff carried one, his wife another. The remainder went to the major-domo of the palace and the leader of the garrison, who was also the foremen of the beaters. The major-domo had been sought, but not found. It was his night of rest, which he often spent in the Street of Whores. The men seeking him would have to search thousands of bedchambers.

The noblemen on the lawn would never learn of this. One of the beaters saw Tar first, sprinting toward the hunting-party across the grass.

"The pit-fighter!" the beater shouted. "He lives!"

Three springbows came up and fired simultaneously. But pit-fighters did their finest work in the open. Tar had dodged countless arrows shot from the stands. He tumbled like an acrobat, the bolts flew through the place he no longer was, and he was running again, the distance now closed. In one hand he brandished a sword, in the other an axe. Both were bathed in blood to the hilt.

In his mind, Tar was fighting before a vast and silent crowd—all those whom he had killed on the shell-sand. They had never lived long enough to seek revenge against the decadent nation that watched them die for petty amusement. Their dead eyes were upon him, and he was going to give them a show.

He hurled himself into the air, and though he did not wear the shining golden helmet, any who had seen him in the arena would know whom he was.

Six boar-spears rose to meet him, and made a fine bridge to the men who gripped them. Although the points cut him, none pierced his flesh. He seemed to dance down the shafts. The beaters were driven to the ground by the impact. Before they reached the grass, two of them were dead. He split another's helmet and blood sprayed like the tail of a fighting-cock. He left his sword standing in the chest of the next.

One of the bearers ran for his life. The one who remained

behind could not run, as Tar had slashed his leg to the bone from hip to knee. Of the three men in plate armor, only the general had gotten his bow reloaded in time.

He fired wildly and the shaft went straight through Tar's left arm. The bolt went on to lodge in the spine of the fleeing beater.

The pain of the wound ought to have slowed Tar down, but it only enraged him. Such men as him turned pain into fuel. He shattered the general's breastplate with his axe, exposing the fine embroidered arming-coat beneath.

"Your Atlantean steel is worthless," said the blood-mad fighter, and with a furious down-stroke, clove the general's entire ribcage in half.

Prince Toba-Ke-Mobi drew his flame-shaped sword, Admiral Sea-Eagle his cutlass of black iron.

"The gods told me I shall only die at sea," the admiral said.

"They are mistaken," Tar growled.

He split the man's pelvis with an up-stroke. The admiral screamed in agony and tried to stop his bowels from spilling out, to little effect. Tar stepped over him and picked up the cutlass. He liked iron blades—a proper metal. He crouched low and faced the prince. It was the fighting stance feared by every pit-slave in Atlantis.

"You should know that I disagree with tonight's miserable sport," the prince said.

"Me too," Tar said through his teeth.

"This is my first man-hunt. I've never seen such pointless cruelty."

The prince was terrified, but the dignity of his birth meant he must face the reckless killer without hesitation.

"*All* cruelty is pointless," Tar said. "But it passes the time."

He lunged, leading with the iron cutlass. Sparks flew as their blades clashed and clashed again. The prince was an accomplished swordsman. But he could only delay his death, and not for long. Despite the weight of the cutlass, Tar carved the air between them with such speed the prince could hardly see it.

"I am not Atlantean," he cried, backing away as Tar drove him across the lawn toward the woods. "I am not your enemy. I am of the Mobi—a prince!"

"I am also a prince," Tar replied. "The Golden Prince."

He tossed the cutlass aside and threw his axe with both hands.

TAR WAS LIMPING, shaking and unsteady as the fury of battle left him. He reached the tree line. At that moment, the door in the hill gave way to the battering-ram, and a mass of soldiers dressed for war came through it.

At the same time, Krait almost ran Tar through with a spear.

She had been lurking near the termite mound, preparing herself for the final fight. When reinforcements came, she intended to make her stand from behind the gate, kill as many as she could, then feed herself to the beasts below.

She had assumed she was alone. Tar would leave her behind once he got into the hill, or die fighting. So when she heard someone coming through the trees, it didn't cross her mind that it might be him.

"Stay your hand!" he yelled.

Her spear stopped inches from his face.

"You're a fucking moron. I told you that before."

"No need to thank me," he said, leaning dizzily against the mound.

All the pain he had denied was starting to make its demands known. He was bleeding from a dozen cuts and his left arm throbbed with every heartbeat as if an army marched over it.

"Why the *fuck* did you return?"

"I missed your conversation."

16

———

Count Liad could hear the crash of the battering-ram across the garden, and then the triumphant shout of many men. He'd seen Tar slaughter the remainder of the hunting-party in the distance, and was impressed. Only a shot as good as himself could stop such a killer. He knew it must be the pit-slave. Legend said he'd slain a thousand men. At close quarters, none could defeat a fighter like that.

He must have pretended to die when the woman stabbed him. It made sense—they thought him dead, so he could come from behind. Working together, the killers had decimated Count Jaff's men and set fire to the woods. That sort of cunning was what made man the finest prey.

He wondered whom of the original hunting-party was still alive. It thrilled him to imagine he was the only survivor. It would make the kill that much more delicious. He realized he had an erection. It pressed painfully against his armor.

"Does it hurt?"

"No worse than a flaying."

"That's too fucking bad."

Krait cauterized the bloodiest of Tar's wounds with applications of oracle lily milk, but if he had been one of her pirate crew, she would have thrown him overboard. She didn't think he'd last until morning with the wounds he bore. They were huddled behind the gate in the entrance to the termite mound.

"I saw many hands of men coming out of the hill," Tar said. "More than we can fight."

"Did you expect to live through this hippo-shit of a night?"

"No," he admitted. "But there are men I still need to kill."

"It's a shame we die here. You'd make a fucking excellent pirate."

Tar felt the old anger return. "Never. It was pirates sold me to the fighting-pits."

"*That's* your grudge against me? Pirates hurt your feelings? " She snorted derisively. "I had no idea you were such a little bitch."

Tears of frustration and rage spilled down Tar's cheeks. He was glad it was so dark— What she'd said hurt more than all of his wounds combined. He groped for his dagger. She caught his hand and pushed the half-drawn blade back into its scabbard.

"Not now. And stop crying, you sniveling titty-baby."

He had forgotten she could see in the dark.

The infuriated soldiers had found Count Jaff's body. Their shouts shook the treetops. They were crashing through the woods, closer and closer. They would soon find the tigers they sought.

Krait was right. Two spears could not defeat a hundred. They were dead already.

"It's time to meet our gods," she said. "Seeing as you're

so upset with me, I'll die first, and then you can piss on my corpse."

Tar laughed through his pain. She was foul-mouthed, vicious, and a pirate. But her spirit never failed.

"To hell with it," he said, and clasped her wrist like a warrior. He drew the master key from his tattered, bloody armor.

"Let's take as many with us as we can."

THE UNDERGROUND CHAMBER where the beasts were caged stank beyond belief. Tar had smelled some terrible things in his life, but this outdid them all. At the bottom of the stairs, he gagged.

"You don't get used to it," Krait said.

There were dozens of whale-oil lamps burning in brackets on the metal walls. Rows of large cages, barred with Atlantean steel, marched down the long chamber. They were divided by a raised mesh walkway down the center of the room. This feature kept their feet above the sea of excrement that ran out of the cages.

Some of the cages were empty—no doubt the result of the day's combat. The rest were filled with monsters. There were giant pigs, reptiles, hunting birds, dire wolves, sickle-toothed lions, hyenas, and creatures Tar had never seen except in nightmares. The animals were agitated—they smelled fire and blood.

As the fighters hurried down the central walkway, the bars of the cages rang with blows of tusks, fangs, claws, and armored hides. The roaring and snarling was deafening. By the time they were past the cages, Tar and Krait were spattered with ropes of saliva.

She showed him a mechanism in the wall at the far end of the chamber, next to a squat door made of overlapping plates of steel. He had no idea what he was looking at—it was a tangle of bronze gears, levers, and wheels. Chains ran from the device, passed through rings in the ceiling, then fanned out to the cages and beyond.

"The ore barges that sail to Atlantis have something like this in their holds," Krait said. "You pull these levers down. The cages open. This one works the gate at the top. These other ones I don't know."

The soldiers had reached the mound above. Their furious shouting rattled down the stairs. Tar shoved the key into the lock on the armored door and twisted it. The lock ground open and the door parted.

"Any time," Tar said.

As the chains pulled tight and the cages clanked open, he and Krait slipped through the doorway. The screams had only begun when the door sealed off all sound. He locked it behind him. They went as fast as he could limp, following the silent passageway that led toward the palace.

Count Liad heard the soldiers charging about in the woods, and wondered if the prey would die before he got the chance to consummate the hunt. It was disappointing.

Then he heard the war-cries turn to screams of terror and pain. He rose a little stiffly—his age had begun to tell— and began the long walk back to the middle of the garden.

The screaming went on and on. It was mingled now with the howls and shrieks of animals. Very large animals. The first trickle of doubt made its way down his spine. He knew those animal sounds; he had silenced every one of them over the years. He'd never heard them all at the same time.

Slaves and soldiers were running pell-mell around the garden. As Count Liad watched, several of them fell through pits beneath the grass. Someone had activated all of Count

Jaff's hidden traps. He stopped walking. Nowhere was safe. He wasn't going to die in a hole in the ground.

Huge, twisted shapes came out of the trees, tearing the human figures apart as they ran, scything down soldiers and slaves. A flaming wolf galloped through the chaos. It fell into a pit, and giant black-bristled spiders—the same type Tar had once faced—spewed out of the pit to escape the flames. When they saw the succulent bipeds fleeing all around of them, they forgot the fire and joined the chase.

It was a hunting-bird that saw Count Liad first. Its round yellow eyes locked onto him and its crest of feathers stood up. Its head dropped low to the ground and it began to run, claws tearing the sod as it picked up speed. The count was master of the situation. He went down on one knee and fired his springbow with perfect accuracy. The bolt disappeared into the keeled breast. The bird crumpled, instantly dead, at which moment the count saw there had been a sickle-toothed lion behind it, stalking. When the cat saw him, it lost interest in the bird. The man was competition for the kill. The man must die. It sprang.

Count Liad didn't have time to reload, so he met the giant cat with his sword. The blade sank up to the hilt between shoulder and neck. Even as the lion died, it plunged its fangs through his sword-arm and collapsed across his body.

The count realized he was not out of danger. Not at all.

He pushed with all of his strength, but couldn't free himself of the carcass that pinned him to the grass. Its jaws had locked in death. He couldn't even cut off his own arm to escape, because his skinning-razor was on his right hip, underneath the cat.

There was nothing he could do but watch as the black-bristled spiders scuttled toward him across the grass, drawn by the smell of new blood.

17

Tar led the way as they emerged into the palace. Krait watched their backs. They were in some minor lamp-lit passageway among the basements. It wasn't decorated or furnished, and nobody was there.

"Everybody's dying in the garden," he said. "This might work."

They hurried along and found a staircase. An elderly woman was coming down with a sack of grain. When she saw the blood-soaked pair, she dropped the sack.

"Kill her," Krait said.

"Excuse us," Tar said.

They ran up the stairs past the old woman. She watched them go, but made no sound. If there was something wrong at the palace, she had no reason to be upset about it. She picked up the sack and went about her business.

They burst through a curtained doorway into one of the lavishly decorated public rooms. The ceiling was worked with intertwined golden octopi, the walls dripping with blown-glass jellyfish whose tentacles were made of strings of pearls. Krait paused to marvel at the opulence around her.

"I am abso-fucking-lutely coming back to rob this place," she said.

"We're getting close," Tar said. "Hurry."

Each of the largest rooms had aisles running along its sides, to accommodate slave activity and discreet meetings. These passages were the safest way to move, as there were many slaves, servants, and functionaries running around the palace. The disaster in the garden had roused the entire household.

Tar cut a lone soldier down, but met no other opposition. The man had been patrolling near the vaulted hall built around the base of the mast. He and Krait ran across this space, their naked feet slapping on the marble floor. The gilded cage that had carried him to Rowana-Ya's private chamber had descending the mast, its chains swaying, and was arriving as they entered the hall. Krait pointed it out.

"What the fuck is that thing?"

The gate of the cage opened. Lady Rowana-Ya stepped out, dressed in her finest skirts and girdle, her breasts sparkling with powdered gold. She had been weeping. Her cheeks were streaked with eye-paint.

When Tar saw her, he forgot their escape. Krait had a more practical response.

"That bitch looks important. Let's kill her."

She charged at Rowana-Ya, but Tar caught her sword-arm before she could strike.

"Not her! She is known to me."

"I know plenty of people, and most of them should fucking die," Krait observed. Tar hung on.

"Kill me if you wish," Rowana-Ya said to Krait.

She had her back to the cage, but showed no fear. In fact, she looked as noble as her pedigree, proud and commanding despite the danger. She spoke now to Tar.

"You have changed everything, although you do not know

it. I watched from my tower and saw the two of you go into the woods. Then the beasts came out, and I guessed you were inside the palace. Now we meet again. There's no time. You have killed the masters of many soldiers, who are entering the palace even now. Get in."

She pointed at the cage.

"Once we're in the tower, we're dead," Tar said.

"This carriage also goes down."

As the cage dropped below the hall floor, Tar thought to introduce his companions to each other.

"Krait, meet Lady Rowana-Ya of house Mannon. Lady Rowana-Ya, meet Krait. She killed your husband earlier."

"I live and die at your command," said Rowana-Ya.

She had no reaction to news of Count Jaff's demise. The three of them rode the cage down through the lowest parts of the palace, through kitchens, storerooms, and slave quarters. Finally it descended among huge machines—pumps, counter-weights, and winches that operated the technologies of the palace. The air was vibrating and booming. At the floor level of this cellar, the cage stopped.

"There is no-one here," Rowana-Ya said. "Come with me."

She took them on a course around the base of the mast. This was its lowermost point. Much of the machinery was dedicated to its functions.

They tucked their weapons in their sashes. Tar found himself staring at the swell of her fine buttocks as the lady strode through that greasy, soot-blackened crypt. He would never forget that afternoon in the carpeted chamber.

Krait, he noticed, was also staring at Rowana-Ya's buttocks.

The pirate woman caught his eye and made a circle of her

finger and thumb. She pumped the index finger of her other hand through it, then pointed at the handsome woman in front of them.

Tar put his finger to his lips. This wasn't the time.

They had circled halfway around the mast—almost a minute of walking—when Rowana-Ya stopped at a small door.

"There is another carriage within. It will take you down to the sea. There is a boat. Inside the boat is a lever. Pull it to go forward, push to go backwards. Upright is stop."

"Why the fuck are you doing this?" Krait demanded, then turned to Tar: "Why the fuck is she doing this?"

Rowana-Ya was looking at Tar, her eyes brimming with tears.

"I call bullshit," Krait concluded. "You're coming with us, your majesty."

She shoved Rowana-Ya through the door. The three of them barely fit in the carriage, which was a windowless metal box. At the touch of a pedal in the floor, they began their final descent.

Tar couldn't understand why she was helping them at such risk to herself.

"Why *are* you doing this?"

"Ah, Golden Prince." Rowana-Ya heaved a ragged sigh, fighting back emotions. "I never fall in love, but it seems I am not immune to severe infatuation. Ever since your escape and capture, I have wondered if you were alive."

Krait pantomimed gagging.

Rowana-Ya mastered her emotions and continued.

"This is the only authentic man I have ever met," she said. "He's damaged, ignorant and violent, but there is an indomitable spirit in him. He is courageous and true."

If Tar was any of those things she said, he didn't feel them. He felt his fresh wounds. His left arm ached like rotten teeth where the bolt had gone through. He felt the suffering of the chain gang and the brutality of the pit. He felt the voyage to Atlantis. He didn't know what kept him alive any more.

Rowana-Ya put her manicured hand to his filthy, blood-stained cheek.

"He has also been the center of a plot. He has no idea, nor did I until tonight. You know that my husband and Heptumu have dealings—to supply animals to the pits. But I recently discovered that Heptumu also supplied my husband with fighters for his hunts."

"He seems charming," Krait said.

"The count wanted to hunt you most of all," Rowana-Ya said to Tar, "but Heptumu wouldn't agree. At last he offered to pay for Heptumu's entire fleet. Heptumu sold you to my husband the same day you escaped."

"So he was never going to let me retire. I thought as much. He wanted me to die in the arena before he lost me. I think it was something to do with insurance."

"He's not *entirely* ignorant," Rowana said to Krait. "Yes, Golden prince. You were worth more dead than alive to your master, until my husband agreed to his price. Then you escaped, and when you were captured, Heptumu had no claim on you any longer. He couldn't use your death to pay for his slave ships or the crew, and my husband got you for free."

"They both sound like consummate dickheads," Krait said.

"One might say that," Rowana-Ya said. "And more."

"But what happened tonight?" Tar asked. "I was busy."

"Your master Heptumu was looking for you after your conviction. He knew you were chained to a pontoon, but not which one. My husband found you first. When Heptumu learned of this, he showed up at the palace in a fury. He confronted my husband while they were watching you slaughter each other before the hunt."

"I knew he was there," Tar said. "I smelled him."

"I knew he was there because my husband forced me to watch the fighting," Rowana-Ya said. "He hated you, Golden Prince. He knew I was obsessed with you. Also, I told him about your penis."

Krait laughed raucously. Rowana-Ya had the grace to be embarrassed.

"When Heptumu realized you were one of the last two fighters standing, he made a wager. It was an act of of desperation. He was going to lose everything. So he staked his entire fortune, all of his property, and a number of things he didn't own on the outcome."

"Then he saw me die," Tar said.

It made sense to him now.

"I saw you die as well, and fled to my tower. As for Heptumu—he fled because he lost the wager."

"I suppose he's escaping on a ship to somewhere," Tar said.

"All this time I have wondered what I could do for you, Golden Prince, to express my affection. Perhaps I am doing it now, for I know whom he dealt with in the harbor, the pirate captain who was to lead his fleet of slave ships. And I also know that captain sails at dawn."

Krait broke in. "That wouldn't happen to be Scimi the Black, would it?"

18

Tar's eyes nearly sprang from his head. If Krait and Scimi were friends, he must kill her immediately. It would be difficult in that tiny compartment. He dropped his hand to the hilt of his dagger.

"How do you know him?" he asked Krait, keeping his voice level.

"That cocksucker took my ship and left me for dead."

Tar let go of the dagger.

"For all of its size, Atlantis is a small place," Rowana-Ya said. "Indeed—Scimi the Black is the man Heptumu will seek. He'll be moored at Kamang Harbor."

The box came to a stop. Rowana-Ya opened the door and a cold, dank gust of air met their faces, heavy with the stench of bilge water. There was a small dock outside, flanked by enormous paddle-wheels that churned the sea to foam. Moored to the dock was one of the enclosed boats Tar had seen while on the chain gang. It bore the three fish of House Mannon on its hull, and it was attached to a cable that ran away among the looming pontoons.

"This gondola will take you to my private docks. I can go

no farther with you," Lady Rowana-Ya said. "My house is masterless and there is pandemonium above. I must take control, or someone else will."

"Fuck that, you're my hostage now."

Krait grabbed the lady's arm.

"I don't think she'd make a good hostage," Tar said, prying Krait's fingers open.

Then he held Rowana-Ya's arm in the same place, but gently. He was unsure of how their previous intimacy affected the rules of good conduct.

"Lady Rowana-Ya of House Mannon, thank you. I can't repay you for this."

"Yes you can, Golden Prince. You can forgive me."

She kissed him on the mouth, cradling his head in her hands. Then she bowed to Krait.

"May the gods favor you…Die with a red blade."

She stepped back into the compartment and closed the door. With a rattle of chains, she was gone.

KRAIT WAS DELIGHTED with the mechanism that operated the boat. She hauled the lever all the way back and the craft shot with sickening speed along the maze of cables.

"This is too fast," Tar said, feeling distinctly seasick. He wished there were windows in the boat's cabin. It was upholstered in sealskin and decorated with panels of rare wood. There were snacks and flagons of wine in a cabinet, all of which Krait consumed. Tar couldn't swallow anything. He didn't want to vomit on the decor.

"Fuck you, this is fantastic. We'll reach the coast in a few minutes. Then we find a ship, stow away, and we can take it over once we're at sea."

Tar felt the hand of his gods in this. Their will pressed upon his mind in a way he could not express.

"Scimi and Heptumu on the same ship. If only—"

"Forget it," Krait said. "You and your fucking revenge, man. Let's just get away."

"Do you know where Kamang Harbor is?"

"I saw it on the charts, but I haven't been there. I know what you're thinking. Drop it, fucknuts. Seriously."

"How close is it to where we're going?"

"Who the fuck knows? I saw it on a map. There are like half a million private docks in Atlantis—a very large number. Get your head right, slave-boy. We are escaping. That's all we're doing."

THEY EMERGED from the boat to find House Mannon's private docks deserted. It was an hour or two before dawn. There weren't even guards on watch. Every armed man in the employ of the family was most likely at the disaster-struck palace. Tar was glad, because he didn't have much fight left in him. It was all he could do to climb out of the boat.

He looked around at the assortment of vessels moored at the docks, which were enclosed by a crescent-shaped artificial harbor.

"We can take that dhow over there," he said. "The two of us could make it go, couldn't we?"

"That pissant little fishing boat? I'd rather eat my own ass."

"This is not the time to be picky," Tar said.

"By the poisonous jugs of the Scorpion Priestess," said Krait.

She was staring away into the darkness surrounding the docks. Tar wanted nothing more than to lie down and sleep for a month.

"Do you see a boat you prefer?" he asked.

"I see a *ship*," she said. "Come on."

· · ·

KAMANG HARBOR WAS next door to the private harbor of House Mannon—the late Count owned the entire stretch of waterfront. Tar followed Krait up a ramp and down a street. There were a few folk about, readying for the day's fishing, but they didn't even glance up at the two soldiers from House Mannon. Soldiers covered in blood were not an uncommon sight, and Krait was tall enough to pass for a man.

Tar was certain of it now: His gods wanted him to see this thing through to the end. They didn't care if he was half-dead. That wasn't their problem.

"There," Krait said.

She pointed out a slim, low vessel at the far side of Kamang Harbor.

"That's Scimi's ship. Look at those lines. She's yare as fuck. Her name is *Barracuda.*"

The ship was bathed in torchlight. Slaves and sailors were coming and going across the gangplank that connected it with the dock, carrying supplies for a long voyage.

"Are you sure it's Scimi's ship?" Tar asked.

He had been trusting Krait's judgment since they left Rowana-Ya behind. There wasn't any particular reason to do so, except he was too tired to make decisions.

"Yes I'm fucking sure. She used to be *mine.*"

They stole along the docks, keeping to the plentiful shadows beyond the torchlight.

"How do you stow away on a ship?" Tar asked. "There are too many people."

"Stow away? Don't be a pansy."

"Then what are we doing?"

There was shouting on the dock near the Barracuda. The fugitives slipped behind a stack of barrels. If they'd been seen, it would go ill.

But as they watched, a nearly circular shape came rushing

down the ramp from the street above.

"Heptumu," Tar whispered.

"Scimi," Krait whispered.

Indeed, it was Scimi who met Heptumu at the bottom of the ramp. The two men were arguing. Heptumu gestured up at the street and waved his arms to amplify his narrative. Scimi listened intently. Then the pirate turned to his crew. He had a proper captain's voice—when he raised it, Tar and Krait could hear him clearly.

"You whale-lice! There's been a change of plans. We're pulling away now. Weigh anchor! Cast off!"

Immediately, the orderly lading of the ship became noisy confusion. The slaves who had been carrying provisions were kicked and cuffed onto the ship. When they weren't beasts of burden, they pulled the oars.

Krait turned to Tar and shook him by the shoulders.

"I know you're well fucked up. I worked by stealth and you were running around like a maniac starting mêlées all night. And I wasn't on a chain gang beforehand, either. So I get it. You feel like hyena shit right now."

"That doesn't matter. Just tell me: what do we do?"

"You're going to hate this."

19

———

Tar was able to swim to the landing-boat tied to the stern of the Barracuda, but he lacked the strength to haul himself into it. Krait pulled him up. Then they lay flat in the bilges and waited for the ship to move. After a time, the slave-driver's drumbeat and the swish of the oars told Tar they were heading out to sea.

He looked up at the blue-black sky, fringed with pink where the sun would soon rise. The Wake of the Night Ship glittered across the heavens. He wondered if his gods had lost interest in him yet. He hoped they had.

"Wake up, shit-lips!"

Tar opened his gummy eyes. It was full daylight. The ship's wake was swirling around their little boat. Krait's face was eager. She couldn't stop grinning.

"You still have your sword? Good. Okay, now we do the thing."

"What thing?"

"Take my ship back."

She hauled on the painter, the rope that secured the boat to the ship, and drew them closer to the stern of the Barracuda.

"Hang on to this," she said.

Tar was so stiff he felt his limbs had been replaced with wooden copies. Disregarding his condition, he took the painter in both hands and pulled to keep the boat in place as she threw herself up over the stern rail. Then she reached down to him.

"Move, numbnuts! Nobody saw me."

They were crouched on the aft quarterdeck behind a heap of provisions that had been hastily thrown onto the ship when Scimi ordered the early departure.

The brilliant sea-light hurt Tar's eyes. He'd spent too much time in the dark recently. But he hunkered down alongside Krait. They had a view of the entire length of the vessel. The galley slaves were seated below the deck, only their heads protruding, with a gangway down the center that joined fore and aft quarterdecks. As the full square-sail drew the ship along at a good speed, the oars had been pulled in and the slaves rested. The pirates, all skilled sailors, set the rigging for the voyage.

Scimi stood at the far end of the ship, looking forward past the figurehead. This was a painted wooden depiction of a barracuda's head, with an extravagant underbite and absurdly oversized teeth. Seated on a cask beneath the figurehead was Heptumu.

Tar was of a mind to draw his sword, charge down the deck, and kill both men at once. Krait sensed this, and held him where he was.

"Do I need to tell you how this fucking works?"

"I kill both of those men," Tar said.

Krait looked him in the eyes.

"I'm a pirate, remember? There are rules."

Tar turned on her, his anger blazing up fresh.

"No there aren't. You do whatever you want as long as it makes you money and somebody dies."

"That's most of the rules," she admitted. "But there's more to it. We have a shitload of unspoken laws among ourselves. Otherwise nobody could get any frigging pirating done."

"Tell me why I can't go kill them."

"If you kill Scimi, these pirates have no captain because you aren't one. They'll kill you in retribution and then fight among themselves until a warship comes along and rams the Barracuda."

"Then what do we do?"

"I'll show you."

Krait stood up, in full view of the entire ship's company.

"Hey Scimi, you worthless cancer on the balls of a dead shitmonger! I challenge you for command!"

THERE WERE a few men in the crew who had sailed with Krait before, but not enough to form a side. Most were old hands of Scimi's. Every one of them stopped what he was doing and gathered on the deck. Even the slaves took an interest, peering over the boards from their low position.

Tar stood up, concealing how stiff he was. Heptumu saw him, screamed, and fell off his cask.

"Do you know that man?" Scimi asked him.

Tar saw that Scimi's once-black beard was now shot through with white strands.

"That's the demon child you sold me years ago!" Heptumu cried.

Scimi took a long look at Tar, ignoring Krait, who stood next to the mast with her sword in her hand.

"You killed my servant and burned down my house," Scimi said to Tar. "I thought you were dead."

"Many people think that," Tar growled.

Krait's fury was growing.

"Scimi, you assfull of rancid walrus jizz: I *challenged* you. Can you not hear?"

"I heard you," Scimi sneered. "What are you waiting for?"

Krait charged down the gangway. Scimi did the same, his sword flashing in the sun. They closed like a chariot crash and fought with such ferocity and speed that it looked as if there were ten swords between them, not two. The pirates shouted and stomped in a frenzy of excitement. They didn't care who won. There was nothing better than watching a couple of hard captains tear each other apart.

Back and forth along the gangway the captains fought. Krait was tired and had wounds of her own, but she was half Scimi's age—and entirely Libagoro.

Tar wanted very much to kill the man who was the cause of all of his troubles. The warm sun was limbering up his body. He'd slept for an hour or two. After all these years, he hated the thought of someone else killing the pirate. But he couldn't assume command, as Krait had told him. Of all the stupid rules to have!

Scimi was tiring, he saw. Krait showed no signs of having fought for her life the last day or two, and as soon as she saw her opponent slow down, she cut him. Then cut him again.

Scimi signaled to someone with his eyes, down in the slave hold. Tar saw three pirates emerge from the shadows, armed with the tridents favored by slavers. Krait couldn't see them. They were behind her.

If he couldn't kill Scimi, Tar thought, then these men would have to do.

With a pit-fighter's howl, he threw himself on the pirates. The first went down with his naked back split open. The others tried to get their tridents to bear, but there wasn't room enough among the slave benches. Tar cut one across the eyes, then hurled his sword at the third. It caught him in the sternum and didn't penetrate enough to kill him, so Tar rushed in and rammed the blade to his backbone. He was pinned to the bench between two horrified slaves.

Tar turned on the screaming pirate whose eyes he'd removed, grabbed him by the loincloth, and heaved him into the sea.

By then, the fight between the captains was over. Scimi was on his backside on the deck with rivers of blood pouring out of his sword-arm. Krait stood over him with the tip of her blade balanced on his vocal cords.

"Do you yield?"

"I yield," Scimi said, his face purple with hatred.

"Should I kill him anyway?" Krait asked Tar.

Blood dripped from Tar's sword, but it was still thirsty. He climbed onto the gangway and stood beside her, looking down at Scimi like he was an unfamiliar species of lizard.

He thought about it. He wanted Scimi to die as much as he wanted breakfast, which was very much indeed. If Scimi died, it would make a fine lesson to the rest of the pirates— not all of them looked pleased to have a new captain.

Then he glanced up and saw Heptumu's terrified face behind the gathered pirates.

"I have an interesting idea," he said.

20

———————

"I don't know how to fight," Heptumu protested.

"You've seen it done a great many times," Tar said.

"Sit on him," Krait suggested.

Heptumu was fiddling with his rings. Tar knew the habit well. It meant the heavy man was hatching a scheme. Scimi's first mate, Skraj, put his own sword in Heptumu's hands. Tar recognized Skraj by the wide, gristly scar across his skull—a gift of the Yunkai. He'd been Scimi's first mate on the fateful voyage to Atlantis, and was one of the only men who hadn't abused Tar during the journey.

Heptumu held the sword as if it were trying to bite him. Scimi's sword-arm had been bandaged and strapped to his chest. He was a skilled swordsman, but not with his left hand. He tested his grip with a few strokes through the air. His opponent didn't know anything about swords except their wholesale price, so it wouldn't matter.

The pirate circled Heptumu, ready to strike.

"Who wins is irrelevant, you gullible fool." Scimi said. "They won't let either of us live."

Heptumu looked imploringly at Tar and began to whimper.

"My honorable ex-slave—and now freeman—promised the winner would be allowed to leave the ship alive."

Scimi was exasperated.

"Look, man. It's obvious I'm going to win this fight. That boy hates me. Look at his face! There's no chance he lets me go."

"Captain Scimi," Tar objected. "I have never broken my word."

"Have you ever *given* your word?"

"Fair point. Die with a red blade."

Money passed hands as betting started among the pirate crew. The men stood in a semicircle around the combatants, shouting cheerful obscenities at the fighters and each other.

Heptumu would surely lose, so they were betting on how many cuts it would take to kill him. None of the money was on the heavy man winning, so Tar bet seven gold serpents he would prevail. He thought that was a suitable sum, as it had been the price Heptumu paid for him. He didn't possess even one gold serpent, so the bet was far riskier than he knew.

The fight began. Scimi feinted with his sword a few times. Heptumu wailed with terror and wiggled his sword vaguely in Scimi's direction. Then Scimi struck in earnest, and blood spilled down Heptumu's flank. The heavy man screamed and began to weep. He farted uncontrollably.

"We're friends, Scimi! Partners! What of our fleet of slave ships? What of the fortune I helped you build?"

"We're standing on the deck of your accursed fleet. And my fortune? Your slave boy and that skinny bitch have it now, along with my command."

He delivered another cut. Heptumu threw his sword aside and dropped to his knees, hands stretched out toward Scimi as if in prayer.

"I beg you, Scimi! You know I did my best! You know I respect you!"

Scimi cut his cheek with another flick of the sword. The wounds were slight, but bled copiously.

"You're the man who ruined me," Scimi said. "As soon as you're dead, these rogues will hack me apart. So I'm going to take my time killing you."

Another cut to the opposite cheek.

Heptumu pressed his shaven head to the deck and crawled to Scimi's feet.

"I beg you," he said, and clutched Scimi's sword hand to stop him from another cut. "I beg you."

Scimi looked boldly around the circle of pirates. Some men he'd sailed with for years couldn't meet his eyes, while others scowled back at him with glee. So it was. Every man with power had friends and enemies.

He turned at last to his rival Krait and the slave he'd taken as a child from the Kohe'Tu river.

"May the Gods curse your souls," he said. "I'll seek you in hell."

He returned his attention to Heptumu, still clinging to his hand.

"I need my sword-hand back, Heptumu" he said. "Otherwise I'll have to kick you to death."

"Don't think you will," Heptumu said.

Scimi shouted with pain and pulled his hand out of Heptumu's grasp.

"You treacherous, stinking—"

His face turned purple. He clawed at his throat, fell to the deck, and his body arched up like a longbow. He quivered like that, every fiber in his body under some incredible strain— and then went limp. He was dead. Several men leapt on Heptumu, beat him unconscious, and stripped the rings from his hands.

"Here it is," said First Mate Skraj. "A ring with a worm adder's tooth in it."

"Poison is a girl's weapon," said a pirate with a neck twice as wide as his head.

"Say what?" Krait said, putting her hand to her ear as if she hadn't quite heard.

"I said poison is a churl's weapon, Ma'am. Sir. Captain."

"I won the bet. Pay up, gentlemen, or be cursed by Iri-Tu-Ko," said Tar, and took fistfuls of coins from the pirates who had bet on Scimi.

"It's not fair!" said one of these. "You *knew* he had a fucking poisoned ring!"

"I guessed it—which isn't the same thing," Tar said. "When I was a pit-slave, he used to come to the Golden Prince's cell to drink wine. All by himself. He wouldn't do that without some hidden means of defense."

"You knew the Golden Prince?" the pirate said, his quarrel forgotten. His face was stretched with awe.

"Like a brother," said Tar. "We fought in the same fights."

21

——————

A bucket of seawater revived the blood-soaked Heptumu. Then he was marched to the gunwale by a cheerful crew. The pirates hadn't been this entertained in ages. Krait put her hand on Tar's shoulder.

"Tar Yunkai," she said. "Be reasonable. Let us skin this sack of boiled assholes alive, *then* throw him overboard."

"I oppose torture," Tar said.

"What a fucking bore," Krait said, and spat on the deck.

Heptumu wrung his hands together.

"You are merciful! But I'm not a strong swimmer, you see, and—"

Tar picked up an empty keg.

"Take this cask to keep you afloat. Atlantis is about fifteen leagues in that direction. You can't miss it."

Heptumu was sobbing by now, prostrating himself at Tar's feet—without the poisoned ring. That meant he was sincere.

"Oh for fuck's sake. At least let me stab him a little bit," Krait said.

"I'd get overboard if I were you," Tar said to Heptumu.

The big man rose trembling to his feet. He threw one leg over the main rail, then the other. He was standing on the planksheer that ran the length of the hull, his slippered heels dangling over the water. He looked imploringly at Tar again. Tar smiled blandly and threw the cask into the sea.

"I'm counting to three," Krait said, and picked up a boarding spike.

Heptumu looked at the hard faces around him, trying to find some way out of his predicament, but there were no allies to be found.

"Three," Krait said.

Heptumu jumped, splashed prodigiously, and floundered around until he found the keg. He tucked it under his chins and began kicking. Soon he was dwindling among the swells. The excitement was over, so the crew got back to work.

"You shit-for-brains," Krait said to Tar, not unkindly. "What if he actually survives?"

Tar shrugged. He walked up to the bow and leaned on the rail, watching Heptumu paddle away. Krait joined him. The sea was rolling and fresh, the breeze fine and the weather promising. If not for his unfamiliarity with better moods, Tar would have considered himself happy.

Heptumu was almost out of sight, still kicking, when the lookout called from the mast:

"Big fish."

A few hundred feet from Heptumu, three towering fins broke the surface. They left a creamy triple wake. Tar remembered those—he'd seen fins like that when Scimi dragged him behind the snake-headed slave ship.

Big fish indeed.

Heptumu saw the fins bearing down on him. He waved his arms desperately at the ship. He screamed and begged and made promises he could never keep, but was too far away to be heard.

The leviathan passed close by him, then submerged with a flick of its tail that threw sea-spray high into the air.

Heptumu began to paddle toward Atlantis again, much faster this time.

"The shark must have smelled him," Tar said.

He didn't care if his old master survived. The men he hated had lost everything to a slave, and now the slave was a free man. That was enough.

He felt gratitude, but not to his contrary-minded gods. In return for vengeance, they had made him the thing he hated most: A pirate. He was free to spend his gratitude where he wished.

Krait laughed. "It's not over yet."

Even as she spoke, the sea rose up in a dome around Heptumu, then exploded into spray as the mighty shark engulfed the man in its jaws and shot straight up into the air. Half of the fish's prodigious length surged out of the water. For a moment it hung against the sky, teeth flashing like swords, black flanks streaked with foam. Then it toppled with a cataclysmic splash and disappeared beneath the roiling waves.

"Never gets old," Krait said.

Tar was grateful to foul-mouthed Krait, bold Lady Rowana-Ya, and gentle Motia. He was grateful to be alive.

Krait was staring at him.

"By Ootah's carnivorous snatch—are you crying *again*?"

"Tears of joy," Tar said.

Here ends the first tale.

ABOUT THE AUTHOR

Fenix 'Nix' Harper-Jones lives in northwestern France with her dogs, Albert and René, and a hostile goose named Edith Piaffer.

When she isn't writing, Nix spends her time restoring an old, long-neglected farmhouse, initiating disastrous romances, and conducting site surveys for l'*Institut National de Recherches Archéologiques Préventives*.

Nix has written many pseudonymous essays, opinion pieces, and poems in French and English. *Slave of Atlantis* is her first novel.